PUMPKIN TEETH

STORIES

TOM CARDAMONE

LETHE PRESS
MAPLE SHADE NJ

This trade paperback published by Lethe Press
118 Heritage Ave, Maple Shade, NJ 08052
www.lethepressbooks.com
lethepress@aol.com

Printed in the United States of America

Book Design by Toby Johnson
Cover art by Kitholeo Lai
First U.S. edition, 2009

ISBN 1-59021-132-4 / 978-1-59021-132-8

"Lightning Capital" first appeared 2005 in *Suspect Thoughts Journal*
"Bottom Feeder" first appeared 2005 in *Outsider Ink*
"The Yolk" first appeared 2008 in *Madder Love: Queer Men and the Precincts of Surrealism*
"Suitcase Sam" first appeared 2005 in *Red Scream Magazine,* 2006 in *Velvet Mafia*
"Mishima Death Cult" first appeared 2004 in *Velvet Mafia*

To those who listened
The few who believed
And the one who knew

TABLE OF TEETH

LIGHTNING CAPITAL

Walking the shore at night I typically stay close to the waterline; condominium lights illuminate the foam of the softly crashing waves. Summer rain sweeps the entire beach clean of footprints, making mine fresh and deep, to mark a meandering road, one that will also disappear, wiped away by early morning high tide. I've been walking the beach a lot lately, thinking about school, about my parents, about Travis, about everything. Mostly I think about Travis. In the distance cloudy remnants of a storm hovers low over the Gulf, flashes of lightning shimmer off the plane of black water.

My parents will want me home soon. Reaching down for a shell I discard my first choice as too concave, clumps of moist sand drop from the cleats of grayish-dusty purple barnacles hidden on the reverse side. Spotting a sturdy chunk of sea glass I scoop it up. It's good and flat and dark green. I imagine it's the bottom of a champagne bottle broken against the bow of a ship launched before my parents were born, rolled smooth on the seafloor by the very waves that eventually, carelessly, pulled down the ship and it's crew, massaging rust into stilled propeller, now scrubbing and caressing the captain's skull, a rotting pipe bobbing between loose, white teeth.

A clap of thunder interrupts.

I skip the chunk of sea-glass across the water, it bounces three times on the tips of stunted waves, to waft and sink back toward its rightful dark playground of seaweed and shipwrecks and diplomatic manta rays.

Yesterday Travis and I rode our bikes to this very spot. He's the only friend I've made since my parents moved us to Siesta Key. We were unloading our U-Haul in front of the new house. Mom, hands on her hips, squinted at the brief yard of white pebbles flecked with Formica–a few loud cactus-looking plants burst forth on either side of the cracked driveway. I knew she was perturbed that we were moving again and likely perplexed that our house had this stony Martian landscape in place of grass. Every time Dad and I passed between the house and the U-Haul he shot me a loaded look, *Help me make this work, Tom.* I wanted to laugh, finishing his thought: *Because we're running out of houses!* But I didn't laugh, I didn't smile. I did not answer his searching, tired, hopeful eyes with mine. This move meant a new middle school. It meant I was far from the few friends I'd managed to hold onto through the last few, towns, the sudden moves.

As dusk neared some kid rode past. Long brown hair hung low in his eyes, barefoot and shirtless, hunched over the handlebars of a dirt bike. Red shorts bunched high on his tanned thighs, clinging like a furled sail. I watched him circle, come back and stop by our new, eager mailbox just as my Dad handed me my own bike from out the back of the truck.

"Hey," he called out. His voice was deep, deeper than mine. I was self-conscious. "Want to go for a ride?"

With that he put both feet on his peddles and rocked his bike back and forth, an urgent balancing act, a rocket about to launch. I wavered.

"Waitaminute," Dad grunted and dug into his pocket. Handing me a ten-dollar bill, "Get yourself some pizza and let your Mom and I unpack."

I shrugged. The unexpected money, this kid on his bike, Mom warily kicking at the gravel–I had no choice. Exhausted from moving, but by now it was all I knew, frustrated, surprised at the burden of tears welling up in the corners of my eyes, I hopped on my bike and sped past the boy. He caught up quickly as I peddled down the middle of the street, trying not to look at him, wandering about the different kinds of dread stuffed into the quiet, flat-roofed houses that lined the block.

"Hey. Let's go back the other way. The laundry mat by the grocery store has the best video games."

He braked. I slowed. "C'mon, I'll show you around." A halo of cicadas buzzed around the sound of his voice.

He told me his name. I said mine softly, a cussword in church. So we swung around and rode silently past my new home. Mom, crying, swung a shovel at one of the cactus-things in the yard, slicing it in half. Dad came up from behind her and tried to take the shovel away. As they struggled I peddled like mad, Travis sped up ahead of me, leading the way. A flock of churlish starlings teased a tilting telephone pole, black against the pink chalky sky.

This part of the beach has fewer condominiums and hotels, more low dunes sutured with stiff brown grass. At night this stretch is darker, quiet. You can hear the sea and you can hear yourself. You can also see more stars but it's harder to see shells so I just stare at the horizon.

This morning Travis crashed his bike through the back yard; feet off the pedals he leapt, letting it drop to skid beneath the grimy dirt bedding beneath the grapefruit tree while he marched into the kitchen, the screen door slamming behind him.

"Hi Miss-us V., got any juice?" He'd already opened the fridge. Bent over, those same red shorts shift, weathered but still vibrant, two sails now stretched full and round. Later we tried try to best our last high score on Frogger at the laundromat, the smell of warm cotton wrapped around us, the drone of churning dryers emitting the white noise of an electric swamp. Pixilated traffic crushed pixilated frog. His turn. I eyed the perfect, red bullet hole heavy on his thigh, a quarter caught between his flesh and taut pocket. Thunder rumbles overhead–brings me back.

A flash of lightning illuminates the slow billowing folds and enlarged corpuscles of a surprisingly low cloud. I turn to cross the beach–to search for a path among the dunes that will lead me to the road.

Another flash but no thunder.

And a star falls.

Skips like a luminous shell, searing the water as it spins.

I smell acrid, saline steam. *That's not a star, it's a...a man? A small body?* I want to comically rub my eyes as the falling star hits the sand at my feet with a gentle thud. I look around. I want an errant jogger, a wino, some Canadian tourist, someone-anyone to verify the beautiful light smoldering at my feet. *A meteor?* It crackles. I squat to look closer. The crackling sound is sand fusing to glass, separating from the cooler, moist sand beneath it with a snap.

The falling star is a little man, aglow, but fading.

No, the little man is a falling star.

I note tiny limbs that end in black points. A chest heaving, he's tired. Wounded? A tiny head, a point really, rising from between an assumption of arms. No eyes, no facial features, but I sense a mouth, a thin dark crease moaning quietly, the only break in the constant glow of his body and limbs, drawn in pain. Not realizing that I'd gotten so close, I feel no heat. But he senses me. His small pointy arms wave me closer. *Impossible.* I freeze, a silent cry reverberate throughout my skeleton. Instinct takes over and I scoop my hands under the soft sand beneath him, bits of broken shell sparkle like jewels imbedded in the fresh glass. Taking the fallen star to my chest I let him feel my fearful heartbeat, confused and rapid. I hold him there and look up, searching for his home. The sky is intermittently black, a fast petroleum pool pricked with the ice of stars, smeared with clouds, but I cannot find an empty space, a hole, a ruptured and blown-out bracket. All is as it randomly should be. The weight in my hands pulses and I lean in without a thought and place my lips over the point I assume is his head, the thin line I believe a mouth; lightly, I breathe out. Injecting my life into his I think, *Thank God this isn't burning my lips.*

So light shoots down my throat.

The skin beneath my fingernails sizzles and glows a wholesome pink. Sparks shoot out from underneath my toenails, tickling the sand. Embarrassingly, my testicles rise, it's like they're rotating in the tight canvas of my ball sac. My hand drops instinctively to cover myself. Every hair on my body stands. Every pore hums.

Revived, the falling star whispers to my entire being, *I am lightning. I am alive and so are you.*

Lightning.

I blink. Hot, molten tears stream down my face. They fall, little drops of brilliant gold burrow calmly into the mess of my footprint.

Thank you. I must fly now. And so can you.

Mr. Lightning hops from my hand and burns on the beach. With a quick, miniature tornado-maneuver he launches skywards. And thunder claps and he's gone. Again I look, pleadingly, for witnesses, better yet, for some kindly old lady to arrive and take me by the elbow and explain everything that just took place in a simple and wise voice. I look up but the sky still looks like the same vast blanket always out of reach. I stand frozen, for how long I don't know, until a rain drop strikes my cheek, then another and another and I run toward the road.

At breakfast my Mom remarks, "Wow, you really are getting a good tan this summer."

I almost choke on my oatmeal. Searching for something to say, I'm relieved to hear Travis' bike clink and whir its way through the backyard. The screen door slams. Lately Mom has been playing a small portable radio in the kitchen. Music is new. She's not as stressed; I'm not seeing chunks of her hair clutch the shower drain. I think it's because we have the house to ourselves. Dad leaves early; he's taken a job delivering papers before dawn all along the Key, coming home to nap before going to the Marriot. He's a line cook for both the lunch and dinner shifts. Checkered pants on the bathroom floor infused with the heavy smell of grease, a white shirt blackened with hand prints across the stomach, the only proof that he lives here.

Whistling to the radio while chopping vegetables she nods to Travis. He grabs a juice and pulls up a chair next to mine.

"Let's go to my house." This is an unusual request.

He looks serious though, so I nod consentingly and wolf down the rest of my oatmeal. He follows me back to my room and leafs through the paperback books on the bookshelf above my battered desk. He is wearing a gray concert T-shirt, another heavy metal band I've never heard of. I only have cassettes; he has his Dad's albums and some of his own. Our tastes are different but he's respectful, acting interested in my music, listening attentively, asking questions. Yesterday at 7-11 he pointed out that the Eurythmics, a band I'd only just turned him onto, were on the cover of *Spin*. Still, his taste seems serious, *older*; in his room, Black Sabbath albums are reverentially separated from the pack and lean against the wall beside a world-weary Jimi Hendrix, the yellowed sleeve peeking out like an un-tucked shirt.

Leaving Travis in my room I go and change my clothes in the bathroom and think about last night. *How did I fall asleep?* I can't recall going to bed, or walking home. I look in the mirror above the sink. My hair is less blonde and more the white center of flame. Hazily remembering dreams of racing clouds, I wonder if these thoughts could be memories. Forcing my mind to veer from the mysteries of last night, I search the pockets of Dad's soiled pants on the floor and find enough money for lunch and some quarters as well. Maybe we could ride our bikes over the bridge and into town. The pizza place off of Route 41 has new video game tables, so you can play while you eat. *Dig-Dug* and *Asteroids* and our knees to touch lightly in the cool air-conditioning.

Brushing my teeth, I think about *Asteroids*–imagining that I'm the laser beam, one with perfect aim, lightning fast.

Travis lives with his father on the second floor of a duplex paneled with dark wood, surrounded by thin Australian pines, a red Camaro permanently parked on cinderblocks in the side yard, itching silently under a layer of decaying pine needles. We park our bikes under the stairway and go up to his apartment. Travis has never mentioned his absent mother. I have never asked.

In his room Travis tells me about Led Zeppelin as he puts on the album. We normally listen in silence. Today, however, he looks at me conspiratorially.

"My Dad's in Tampa today, so I *know* he won't be back until late tonight because he gave me money for dinner."

With a wild grin, he shoots out of the room. I hear him rummaging in his father's room. He returns with a worn paper bag. We sit cross-legged on his bed while he coolly pours out the contents: *Hustler, Penthouse, Playboy*. All of them so well-thumbed the staples in their spines have expanded; the pages hang loose and shifty, ready to slap our faces. My cheeks are red with embarrassment as the curiosity seething in my pants pins me to the bed.

"Fuck the pictures, man. I love reading the letters."

He quickly picks up *Penthouse* and leafs toward a remembered, savored section. I am left to grope through the remnants of a *Playboy*. What I really want is *Hustler*. I know men lurk inside, but want to approach these wild, hairy animals surreptitiously, my aim shouldn't be apparent, at least not yet. As I methodically review the women in my magazine and pretend to size up their uninteresting breasts, I steal glances at Travis. The magazine in his lap obscures his magical shorts, eclipses everything the magnet in my heart pulls me toward. Lamely I let *Playboy* drop and pick up *Hustler*. Opening the magazine to the middle, a shiny and creased page reveals a naked man staring intently at the pink bull's eye between the parted thighs of a woman sprawled over the edge of a bed. Her tits roll, milky arms back, hair flowing with the shape of the sheets…but *he* was solid. His stomach a series of blonde steps tumbling down, folds of muscle twisting beneath a patch of furious, blind hair, rising as a single point of …I close the magazine and look at Travis. He's looking at me.

"Hot stuff, huh?"

He puts his own magazine aside and leans back on his elbows, crossing his ankles. The internal arch against his shorts is strong. He looks toward his stereo.

"I'm gonna flip the record."

He's off the bed in a flash. *Those red shorts.* I keep my magazine in my lap. Equally tight, his t-shirt barely reaches his shorts, brushing the waistline like tattered palm frond. Bits of color flitter across its back, tour dates maybe, long washed away, the fabric worn to a cloudy gray. If I could put my hands underneath his shirt, absorbing the heat from his chest, fingertips skating across smooth skin, gathering kinetic energy…I want to pull at my shorts and adjust my tense erection but I'm afraid to touch myself. Light might pour out.

My toes *do* feel hot. I glance down; they are glowing, slightly, just under the nails, a bright warm yellow. *Shit.* I tuck my feet under my ass and pretend to stare at the cover of the magazine. Travis sits back down on the bed and takes off his shirt. His tiny nipples are sharp and close together, his stomach looks like the young, ready wood that the abdomen of the man in *Hustler* was carved from. Sitting at an angle, with just the cusp of his buttocks on the bed, legs out straight, toes barely grazing the carpet, I can see how the power of his erection draws the taut shorts even further up his thighs, exposing white tan-line, the shocking border I desperately want to cross. I know I am the first person to ever see this glance of tundra.

"I was reading the letter in *Penthouse* about this guy who gave this other guy a blowjob. I mean, David Bowie's bisexual." He glances at his record collection.

"I guess I'd let a guy suck my dick. But it would have to be someone I know really well. And I don't know if I could be friends with him again, you know? It's like a trade-off, something that could only happen once."

He looks at me curiously. I'm seeking but not finding lust or doubt on his face. The hair on his forehead hangs in thick, unwashed strands. He looks at me the way I must look at the ocean at night, a thoughtfulness that in unconcerned with possible replies.

My toes are on fire, heating my ass. Worried I might burn holes in his bedspread, I croak, "Let's swim –race you."

I was off the bed and out the door. I heard it slam rapidly behind me. Travis' place is across the street from one of the smaller public parking lots that access the beach. My body unleashes a speed I have never felt before–looking back I smile, my fear and longing replaced by pride. Struggling to catch up, a look of determination screws his face. With the beach in sight I feel the asphalt beneath my toes soften, every so slightly, as I race toward the rolling waves.

We swim for hours, crashing our bodies into the surf, forcing explosions with our shoulders, forming slinky brown torpedoes riding waves ashore. Finally exhausted, thirsty, we walk back to his house, gulp water from the green garden hose coiled on his neighbor's porch. I get my bike while he takes a drink. I don't want to go upstairs again. Not yet. Bike mounted, I coast out onto the street. It's rare for me to take the lead but Travis follows. Rare, too, for me to ride with my shirt off, the coolness of the salt water clinging within the hair at the base of my neck contrasts with the heat building on my cheeks and shoulders. As we ride I check my fingers and toes; everything seems fine.

Keeping my head low as we cross the drawbridge, I watch the rush of boats beneath us; the center portion of the bridge is a metal grid. The wind is more serious at the high point and I don't want my eyes to tear; I worry my tears might be flammable. Flying off my cheeks one of my molten tears might whip over my shoulder and strike the spokes of Travis' bike and send him tumbling over.

After dinner, while my parents watch *M.A.S.H.*, I go for another walk on the beach. I always tell them I'm walking up to the 7-11 to get a Slushie. I want to retrace my steps. If I'm lucky, or find the right spot, maybe I can talk to the lightning.

It rained late in the afternoon, typical of a Sarasota August. Once again the sand is free of footprints, in their stead millions of pinpricks, indentations to match the stars in the sky, seen and unseen.

I'm disappointed that the sky is so clear.

Still, I feel light on my feet. Remembering how fast I ran in the morning, I jog down the beach for a bit. The balls of my feet beg for greater speed. My arms demand, ridiculously, that I lift them above my head like a diver. I obey my body and transform. *Like liquid.*

Lightning fast.

I shoot skyward.

Every molecule neatly realigns into the arrow I have become.

An arrow of light.

Speeding toward a cloud so high it was nearly invisible from the shore I see Siesta Key recede below, its sister islets become visible. Bridges become toothpicks. The city un-spools as unsymmetrical rows of faint Christmas lights.

In the cloud I coil. So. The cloud is our nest. I see other shocks of lightning bounce around, buzzing about me, about each other, about where to strike and, of course, buzzing about the weather.

A massive spark approaches. I knew it's my fallen star from last night. Its voice a rapid pulsating light I understand.

Without even meaning to, I flash my response. I understand. I saved your life so you saved mine. I can fly anywhere–ignite forests with the heat of a star. With a burst of light I know to be a smile he is off.

Down, down, down, the metal of the earth is so attractive, so demanding, I have to follow.

And I hear the close snap of thunder and think, *That must be me.* I land a mile from our house, on the tip of the island, where the few homes are obscured by a mass of Australian pines. Occasionally the sand here is roped off in square patches to protect a clutch of turtle eggs. I sit in a seared hole of charred glass, my bottom cool against slippery glass formed by my descent. *How long have I been sitting here?* My arms feel strong, my calves tight and happy; this is the feeling I get after racing my bike over the bridge, stung by the marvel of all of the life streaming below. Rising, dusting myself off, I walk home. Staring at my fingertips, they seem ready to ignite. Craving the sky, I know enough to go home. I don't want to get into trouble.

Travis drops his bike in our backyard and slides into the house behind my mother, who is returning from the garage with a laundry basket.

He rummages in the refrigerator. "Hey Miss V., we're getting the VCR back from the repair shop tonight. Is it okay if Tom stays the night?"

Mom shoots a "Sure" over her shoulder as she disappears down the hall.

I'm staring at Travis, dumbfounded he didn't mention this to me before. Drinking orange juice from the carton, he winks at me.

Before we're out of the yard on our bikes he pulls close and whispers excitedly that his Dad has to work late in Tampa again and won't be coming home.

We turn out onto the street. A small grass snake struggles vainly in the cement gutter. "And I found a bottle of rum under the sink. I just *know* he's forgotten about this one. We can drink rum-and-cokes!" And with this he pops a wheelie, launching his front wheel high into the air, a charioteer about to charge the sun.

When I got home last night I unearthed the encyclopedia set from among the boxes still in the living room and read about lightning. Florida is the Lightning Capital of the world with more lightning strikes here than anywhere else. The chances are greater that you will be struck by lightning than win the lottery or get bitten by a shark. Both happen in Florida with certain regularity, it's just that lightning strikes are more frequent. I remember how my sixth grade social studies teacher, Mrs. Rathke, was struck and killed by lightning while she walked a beach with her twin sister. It was a sunny afternoon, not a cloud in the sky, when just as they passed another pair strolling down the beach, lightning struck. What made the papers all over the country was a man, passing by at that exact moment, also happened to be a twin with his brother. I would often imagine both cauterized twins standing over their dead doppelgangers and looking out into the blind eye of the Universe. Mrs. Rathke had been my favorite teacher. The entire class cried as the substitute teacher wrote his name on the board.

That same year a golfer was struck by lightning. That happens a lot. He survived, which also happens. However his zipper was fused to his dick. I wondered about that a lot, too.

We also have in Florida *ball lightning*. It's no urban legend, but lightning grabbing itself by the knees and getting ready to roll. This is lightning that's just not in much of a hurry. Rare, for sure, But true nonetheless.

The next time I'm in the clouds, I'm going to talk about Mrs. Rathke. I'm going to tell everyone to be more careful. I will say her name loudly, but all you will hear is dark thunder.

At Travis's house we watch movies and slowly sip strong rum-and-cokes. His father *had* picked up the VCR from the pawn shop, so that was cool. We rented *Evil Dead.* I don't know if it was the alcohol, my new experiences in the sky or Travis' knee close to mine, but when the demon in the movie speeds through the forest I push myself back against the couch, bracing for impact. The film hypnotizes Travis. I could have touched him, if I dared.

I'd taken one of my Dad's cigarettes–I could only get away with taking one. He counts them, smoking a pack-a-day, finishing the last one at midnight with Johnny Carson, starting a fresh pack in the morning, before the sun comes up, as he pulls his car out of the drive.

Afterwards we go to the beach. Low tide. The sand by water's edge is compacted and hard. We leave our flip-flops at his house and wade out until the water laps at our knees. Travis tries not to cough–I try not to look at the horizon. Ignoring the sky is painful. A wave a little bigger than the rest slaps my cut-offs; absorptive cotton tendrils lie heavy on my leg. He passes me the cigarette and I take a hit. It burns the sweet, thick film of rum off my tongue. Travis is looking down into the water–I notice a slight radiance gripping our feet–I panic. *I'm doing this.* But he reaches into the water and makes glowing trails with his hands. There's an algae bloom in the tide that's phosphorescent–I try to write my name in the water, of course it doesn't work but Travis figures out what I'd doing and grins.

We make more rum-and-cokes and take them back to his room. He plays Pink Floyd, some of their early stuff, and explains the importance and the difference between this and the hugely popular later albums, but I'm only half-listening. I look to my toes, worried that when I open my mouth my tongue will shine in his eyes like a flashlight. Travis senses I'm uncomfortable and thinks it's my wet shorts. I'm sitting on the floor trying to understand the importance of a cow on one of the Pink Floyd album covers when Travis comes back into the room with a towel. He hands it to me and tells me to go outside and hang my shorts out to dry on the railing. Outside I pull down my shorts. At least my underwear is kinda dry. The night air feels wondrous and new on my skinny legs. And familiar. Like I'm flying. Again. So I grip the railing, worried that I might shoot off into the sky. I could use the towel as a cape. No, it would probably burn up. I wrap it around my waist and go back inside.

The lights are off. A single stunted candle burns on a plate in the middle of his room. Its quivering light dimly paints the walls into a shifting cavern. *I like this.* I sit next to Travis on the bed. He is sprawled out against a wall of wilted pillows.

"Too bad you couldn't score another cigarette."

"Yeah, I know. I'm flying with this rum."

"Yeah. Me too."

Travis rolls over and I can see he's in his underwear. I look around the room for his red shorts. There they are, like a deflated hot air balloon crashed in a forlorn field. Lifeless and sad, their color has gone out. The towel feels leaden, false. I take the last sip of my drink and take it off. Neither of us moves. I can feel the hair on my thighs rise. Energy sparks invisibly at my elbows. My underwear tightens at the crotch. I will speak fire.

"Travis… I-I-I think I'm made of lightning."

The record stops.

"I know what to do," he replies, then gets up and leaves the room.

I sit there and think about what he said the day before. I wonder if this is the last time I'll ever be in his room. In the candle light the red shorts look like a giant dead leaf. Travis comes back into the room.

"Follow me."

He leads me into the bathroom. Water is running. The mirror is white, the tiny room moist with hot fog. Travis opens the shower door and steam pours out. He slips off his underwear.

"C'mon, I want to be your cloud."

I dive in.

I'd promised my parents I would go home for breakfast. In the kitchen everything is different. It's like we've moved again but instead of trading neighborhoods I have somehow moved into myself. The chair feels different; the apple scent of my gluey oatmeal is alive. I'm starving and shovel it down. It's without regret that I don't expect to see Travis. I'm okay with it but I wonder how I'll spend the day. Putting my bowl in the sink the doorbell rings. Mom answers and its Travis, loaded down with two brown Publix grocery bags filled with oranges, the hurricane maps on their sides buckling and bending, distorting the grid wrapped around Florida. He tells my surprised and pleased mother that his landlord lets them pick the trees behind their duplex. Mom takes one bag into the kitchen while he follows with the other.

"Let's take some to the beach." I agree and rush to brush my teeth.

And we are mermen, fishboys, cutting the waves with our bodies all morning long. I notice the white sheath of his underarm when he cuts a wave, arms raised, hair braided with salt, bits of seaweed twisting around his neck. We swim out to the sandbar and feel for sand dollars with our toes, treading water when a larger wave lifts us. His hand on my shoulder as we rise with the wave is a wave of its own and I relax, willing to let this new tide take me, weightless, wherever it will. I notice slight reddish burns on his shoulder…my fingerprints. We're going to have to be careful.

For lunch we get Slushies, hotdogs and chips at 7-11 and eat in the parking lot, bikes splayed against a haughty banyan tree, its trunk mauled and sliced by the various fenders of careless drivers.

After dinner I sit on the edge of my bed. When my parents settle in front of the TV I'll go for my walk. But this time I will run faster down the beach. I will run and will myself into the sky again, but I won't strike aimlessly, I will gather myself and bounce from cloud to cloud, pinball across the ocean, writing my name large and clear.

Pulling on my sneakers, I didn't hear the ring but I can hear my Dad's voice, loud and reactionary on the phone in the next room. He's telling my mother something as I stand up, ready to head to the beach. I can feel the sparkle grow at my elbows. The slightest hint of radiance emanates from the worn rubber soul of my sneakers when my parents angrily enter my room.

"That was Travis' father on the phone."

The spark racing up and down my forearms dissipates.

"Apparently he wasn't even home last night."

My toes go cold. Ten little light bulbs break.

"And that you boys consumed alcohol."

Their hands are actually on their hips. I can no longer feel it, the magnetic pull of the earth. Or Travis. I think about opening my mouth and letting fire shoot out to burn them before they steal my new powers -and then in unison they say it:

"YOUNG MAN,

YOU.

ARE.

GROUNDED."

BOTTOM FEEDER

Yes. Stick your whole fist in. My massive form gyrates underwater, turning on the fulcrum of your divine fist. A delicate flap of the small flippers that replaced my legs sends me spinning slowly, like the gigantic propeller of a grand ocean liner. Even in the hyper-controlled environment of the Tank I still get the occasional barnacle. The pool boys who bring us our meals are quick to unfasten the knives from their skinny hips and pry them loose. Pool boys. Lovely pool boys, wee skinny lads with bright green skin, thin arms and long, webbed fingers, they love to swim circles around our loose-knit pod. They love to tease us by tossing the more succulent cabbages to and fro while we salivate, thickening the water before us. Speaking of which, where is lunch? I am several pounds of seaweed and cabbage overdue. Still, the pool boy with his arm immersed in my gulping anus provides a wondrous, tickling distraction. I pause my slow-motion cycling and allow him to push further in; my cavity contracts around his tight fist, tiny explosions of sensation, starfish kisses, blow through my blubbery midriff. And here come the cabbages! Rolling toward us like gourmet depth charges.

With a quick clap of my flippers I propel myself forward, expelling my submariner servant. Nibbling at a round of cabbage small specks of vegetable matter tumble away, fodder to the small fish that share our tank, behind me the pool boy floats forlorn, massaging his uncaged arm.

Life in the Tank, you ask? It's going just swimmingly, dear. Bliss, a living dream. I float. Float and dine. The cabbages are plump and firm yet come apart in my mouth like giant truffles. And the pool boys. How they swarm about me. I roll in their precious little arms, strong arms, excavating arms, I dare say. The joy in a proper enema-that one lad, I love how his blonde hair wavers above his head in the water like a fan of precious coral; I didn't even know he was in until the knob of his elbow elicited a small shudder within my buttocks. You have to be careful, you know. Going in without our full acknowledgement can be dangerous. I've heard of lost limbs. Our sphincters are sizeable. Nearly as big as our appetites. *But the Tank. It's huge, of course. Huge. I once saw it from the outside, in fact. A rare experience among my fellow denizens, some of which, I hazard, do not know which city we are in, or that we are even in a city. There are those who have been in the Tank so long they have forgotten it is, indeed, a Tank. They have given themselves over to the illusion in its entirety. We have a phrase for this phenomenon, those who have so completely disassociated themselves from their past are said to be in "open water."*

Lucky lucky lucky. I'm sure some of them are faking. I'm sure others are not. That big lumbering ox over there, I call him the Professor. Largest of the pod, thick whiskers undulating below his puffy jowls, he's rumored to have been here the longest. I wouldn't know. No one would. We do not speak of the past. We do not share names, nothing to ruin the surrender, the drift. After all, we are all heading for "open water," are we not? Why spoil the ride.

But I came different. I was not yet among the impossibly rich. But I was close, close to them anyway, I followed them like a pool boy, netting discarded trinkets in their wake. No, worse than that. I was a bottom feeder, filtering their shit for morsels of value, groveling for favor. That is what led me to the Tank. I put one of them here. Well, not physically. As his lawyer I handled the paperwork. Not even that. As his lawyer I hired the accountants who handled his paperwork. I reviewed the reams of release forms he had to sign for legal flaws. That's where my interest grew. That they could promise such things, take such fortunes and still deliver. This I had to see. Not that you could see it. The Tank is really a nondescript office building in the old Garment District. It's what's in the basement that is so damned interesting: the largest aquarium in the world. A forgotten underground garage transformed into a vast playground for aquatic voluptuaries, those aristocratic souls grown obscenely bored, having decamped Paris for the moon then back again, still bored. So what's left for the existentially obese? The Tank. The Tank goes further; further retirement, total surrender to the expansion of your baser needs. Here you can become a new being, expanded to fully encompass obscene craving. Afloat with designer taste buds, engineered to thrill at soggy lettuce, somersaulting in your own excrement, the mind appropriately narrowed, focused to fully grasp true need. I helped file all the necessary paperwork. I inspected the site at his request. I saw bloated angels in paradise.

I liked what I saw.

I must have drifted off to sleep. I try to forget that I was once privy to the circumference of the Tank. Not that I knew the exact dimensions. But obviously it could not have more then the length and width of a typical city block. Quite possibly it expanded well under the street, but not for too long, ancient subways likely restricted such expansion, after all. Depth, however, might not have had such limitations. Still, like everyone else here, I feel as if I am adrift within an endless sea. That's part of the design, our design. Among our many neural alterations is a curvature in our sense of direction; all of our movements actually take us at an angle, exaggerating our chosen direction. I could swim deliberately for hours in what I think is a straight line and never come into contact with the concrete wall I know is there. Not all of the changes are so subtle: we are, after all, huge. Wondrously finned for rotation and playful swimming, taste buds teased and excited to the point where everyday cabbage and seaweed elicits the ecstasy of a seasoned gourmand. Sexual ecstasy has been equally enhanced, and rightfully internalized. We are all floating eunuchs in the Tank. Stripped of our sex organs, de-wired, the pesky sensation-seeking nodules and nerves transplanted where they always belonged, up our asses. The ecstasy of eating leads to the ecstasy of excreting. Heaven. Brown heaven. Not that the heft of roughage we put away each day needs much prodding, but the pool boys fancy the idea of a friendly enema by way of the occasional nutritious depository… delicious pool boys knuckling loose my waste, massaging an internal orgasm that sets me spinning for hours.

I whistle a greeting to Ol' Blue Eyes. Singing to himself, he nods a patrician consent. I have assigned names to most of my rotund brethren and wonder if they have done the same. Or does such frivolous nomenclature keep one from reaching "open water?" Who cares? Ol' Blue Eyes simply whistles more than the rest of us, beautifully so, hence the name. Sound travels strangely underwater, looping and turning like blown glass, expanding until what I imagine I am saying actually sounds like an elongated bellow. Yet another change to our brains—we understand each other innately. My first day in the Tank felt like every other day since: fully acclimatized, at ease, a complete understanding of my surroundings. Bliss. I do not think the pool boys understand what we say, however. But they do a good job of smiling and nodding and waving. Look, two of them armed with long scrub brushes, chasing after Ol' Blue Eyes. Lucky lucky lucky. He is going to get a good scrubbing. He'll bask in the attention, but it won't interrupt his song. Of course I have no idea how long I have been in here, but that's the point, *silly.* But since I've been in, and I am comfortable guessing it has been about a year, he has been singing the most exquisite song, full of bursting underwater arias segued between the softest, most sublime interludes, a year long opera of excrement. Ol' Blue Eyes sure loves to shit.

What was my client's name? Oh yes, Norman. Norman. Norman was not going to be a typical Tank Dweller, no. Norman was not looking for underwater nirvana, Norman was looking for a place to hide. Of course I did not know his crime. I knew enough not to ask and Norman had enough respect for my profession not to volunteer any information. Norman needed to hide and knew enough not to go off-world. Everyone who wants to hide goes off-world. Cults are always good, but you still have fingerprints in a cult, or at least most cults, and DNA. No, Norman was smart. He was smarter than me, or at least he knew more about certain things than I did. I had been in the service of the very wealthy for nearly a decade, since law school. I thought I knew everything. Norman showed me that there is a world where the merely very wealthy look like paupers, a world that contains the Tank. And joining the Tank, taking the plunge, as they say, is more then a few days of surgery and deep genetic alteration, more than slicing on a few gills and rolling you into the water. To change your skins' adaptability to water, your organs and whatnot to such a radically different environment, you had to alter a person's DNA, and if or when human form is returned, the slightest of alterations remain. Thus, the perfect escape coupled with a perfect disguise.

Now, like I said, most people who take the plunge do so as a form of further retirement. They are not just bored -they are bored with being human. But there are a few who wish to experience the Tank for only a short while: a year's rest and nothing more. This was going to be me. Or should I say Norman. He transferred a significant amount of money to my account. More money that I ever imagined I would have in my account. And all I had to do was take the plunge. Except that Norman would take the plunge in my place.

The plan was for me to go to the interview wearing a biological hologram of Norman's DNA, so important for identification as well as the procedure. As I exited the taxicab I applied an aerosol that for a short time overlapped my DNA with Norman's. The interview was extensive, but so was my coaching. I had traveled near enough to these circles to easily adopt the attitude of their typical client. I had even ingested a small amount of synthetic heroin for effect. Accepted, I would sign a contract for a year's immersion, a vacation, really, a taste of retirement before I fully commit. Not unheard of. What was unheard of, at least in all likelihood for Norman's sake, was that I *would like what I saw on my initial inspection. Really like it. Like it enough to forgo the biological hologram but take his money. And once payment was made and the date had been set wherein I, or I should say my doppelganger, was to enter the tank, I arrived an hour early and thus before a surely befuddled Norman, changing my contract to a lifetime commitment. I had been holding the door open for rich people long enough. I figured it was time for me to go first.*

I awake floating on my back. I think I dreamed of cabbage. I am not sure, though. A soft curtain of wavering light filters through the green mist, shades of green darken below me, yellowing above me, undulating at either side. A tight spear of small orange fish shoots by. Rolling over I hear Ol' Blue Eyes in the distance, singing lightly in his sleep. A few others have gathered near a fresh crop of cabbage, I swim their way. The thought of dining on fresh cabbage causes my full bowels to quiver in anticipation- imminent release. I pick up the pace. Fat slivers of a new, dark seaweed float among the slowly unfolding balls of cabbage. I deftly slip past the Professor to slurp up an appetizing strand and, finding it to my liking, lap up another. A school of pool boys bob in the distance, waiting to attend us after the feast. My stomach grumbles as my rear yearns for a probing hand.

I wonder whatever became of Norman. I know that the people who were looking for him wanted badly to find him—I hope he knew it was okay to stay at my apartment—I didn't need it anymore. Or maybe he's here. That one over there is kind of new, the big whitish one. I will call him Ahab. Maybe he has already started calling me Ishmael. Who cares? Not like this was the only Tank. I was shocked that there were so many Tanks. Some are off-world, orbiting satellites. Imagine that, circling the planet, a necklace of tinfoil globes filled with designer aquatic mammals excited wholly in their own defecation... evolution is a wondrous thing, is it not? I was further surprised to discover a preserve in Madagascar where one could become a sloth. I guess that was for people who can't swim. Well, I have bigger problems. Today I drifted away from the others; it's nice to just drift, when I thought I saw a shark. I know, I know, impossible. This is the most benign environment in the universe, right? For the longest time I thought it was another member of our pod, on his own off in the distance. But we tend to float about and this shape was stationary. In trying to discern who it was I gave it a hard look, but no matter how hard I tried to see who it was I could only make out the haziest of shapes. As I drifted closer I thought I could see a dorsal fin, black and sharp, poised like a knife. And then there was a sudden shift in the light, green went to blue and then back again, and the shape was gone. And it's not like I can raise my hand to tell the teacher. I don't have hands anymore. And there are no teachers. This is a self-sustained utopia (oh aren't they all?). Swimming quite quickly for my tonnage, I sought the comfort of my indifferent pod.

One more thing about the office building above the Tank, it was nondescript, another boring compendium of glass and not-much-imagination left over from the Twenty-second Century, at first glance, that is. Windows and panels and mirrors and the above-ground floors of the many-storied building existed solely to draw and refract sunlight toward the Tank. A measured amount of light pours in, the rest is stored, reserved for the banished night. There is no night-time in the Tank, just permanent twilight. An emerald sunset pulsates around us, our frolic endless.

No pool boys so far today. Do they have the day off? Is there a holiday specifically reserved for submerged cabana boys? My fat fraternity seems unconcerned, as they should be. Enough deteriorating cabbage still floats about the Tank. I want to dive. I want to submerge deeper into the Tank but every push downward, no matter the strenuous exertion, I find myself relatively even with the pod. But I crave the shadows, the limitless, undefined darkness below. I tire of this lukewarm temperature, this constant constancy; it must be cold below. But surely not safe. A surge of bubbles, white torpedoes descend… here come the pool boys! Wide smiles and long scrub brushes, I roll over. Stomach exposed, I luxuriate in their pending attention. This and some more of that black seaweed will set me singing. A tight spear of small orange fish shoots by.

THE SPHINX NEXT DOOR

Occasionally my neighbor's mail gets mixed up with mine. When this happens I simply slide the envelope under her door. This time it was a package. I could knock; she's always home. But my neighbor is a sphinx and best avoided. All those riddles. At first I imagined she was too large to leave the apartment, but realized this was ridiculous because she would have been too big to fit through the door in the first place, though who can say how much a sphinx grows, or what they eat, although our assumptions of the eternal intuit a certain constancy. *Dieting can not and should not be an aspect of immortality.*

The package was the exact size of a box of checks, and equally nondescript.

I told my boyfriend about this conundrum over lunch. Since I had moved to Brooklyn lunch had become more significant for us, and for me at least, a bit strained. We don't see each other so often anymore. Not unless I stay the night at his place in Manhattan. He refuses to stay over at my apartment and in the three months since I moved he has come over just once, to my housewarming party. That night, he placed the plant he brought as a gift on the kitchen table and launched into an invective against the length of the commute. I ignored it and let my martini settle in. He left early when I'd expected him to stay the night. I had invited the elves from accounting and they arrived late. I wanted to see how he would interact with them; my place is so small it would have been virtually impossible for them not to co-mingle. The party was a success. Friends I hadn't seen in years came. Everyone complimented my new place; even for a studio it is more spacious than most Manhattan apartments. They deposited gifts, bottles of wine and funny napkins, in the kitchen. While I made drinks people looked around, laughing if they had the same Ikea furniture.

We both work in Midtown, so meeting for lunch is easy, routine. I told him the plant he had brought died. "Likely from over watering," he'd said, coolly.

"They have wings, don't they?" He turned his fork. A purple vein of radish slithered between two chunks of lettuce.

"No, that's a griffin." I sipped Diet Coke through a straw, annoyed. He probably knew that, but always feigned ignorance or disinterest when the subject of Faery Folk came up. "Anyway, this is the Post Office's fault. Let them take care of it."

I brightened. He had a way of seeing past a problem, straight through to the solution. He effeminately dabbed the corner of his mouth with a napkin, an affectation he knew bothered me. One eyebrow arched in exaggerated surprise as I paid the bill. He is insistent that we always go Dutch and keep things *even*. I think there's nothing wrong with the occasional exuberance to counterbalance our mutual thriftiness. And I bet deep down he agrees. After all, he's the first man to hold my hand in public. Whenever we cross the street he grabs me, offering a sure hand, watching traffic while pulling me toward safety.

When I arrived home, the package seemed discolored at one corner. An oil stain appeared to be spreading. I held it to the light. *Was it already like this?*

I could wait until the weekend. On Saturday I could explain the mix-up to the mailman, and let him put it in the Sphinx's box. And it was a good excuse to *not* stay at my boyfriend's place. Let him miss me for a change, and maybe motivate him to at least consider coming out to visit me. The mailman is taciturn, however. Rude. Once, in passing, I casually tried to fish out my mail while he sorted letters. He violently slammed the mailbox shut, forcing me to quickly recoil. Holding my fingers in mock-injury I swallowed my complaint as he shot me a withering look.

Was the package this heavy yesterday?

This was a ridiculous error on *his* part. Her mail is addressed so singularly. *Sphinx*. Not even a street address or a zip code. And anyway, the weekend was several days away. I couldn't wait for the mailman.

I took a bottle of cheap wine from the top of the refrigerator and poured myself a glass. Normally I turned on the television when I came home. Instead, I put my ear to the wall and listened. Nothing. I never heard a noise from her apartment, not even the TV, though I imagine she watches *Jeopardy*. I went to uncork the bottle but realized it was a screw-top. The wine scorched my throat.

I wondered if the downstairs neighbors can hear her, if they complain.

I loosened my tie and poured the rest of the wine out of the glass and down the sink, trying to remember who had given me the bottle. The gaudy label was over-ripe with a floral, stylized script in another alphabet... maybe cuneiform?

I tried to recall the difference between sphinxes; Grecian ones are mean. They strangle you if you can't answer their riddles. I think most of the sphinxes in New York are Egyptian, aloof, noble guardians. They tend to work in banks or human resources, if they work at all.

She must go out to get the mail.

I decided to leave the package at her door.

I looked out the ancient peephole. It's oddly nautical, a metallic half-orb with a little lever that opens and closes. The glass magnifies everything. The hall was bright and empty.

Like everyone in the building, I am wary of the cats. The halls are stalked by slender, silken felines with human faces. The real estate agent warned me of their presence in that coy way they always spin things. I remember her showing me the apartment.

"At least with mythological beings you don't get the dander. Allergies are not a problem." Smacking her gum and gesturing broadly, she tried to draw my attention back toward the recently refinished cabinets.

This part of Brooklyn was thick with mystical cats and graveyard dogs. Thankfully I wasn't close to a cemetery. I would hate to live in Sunset Park and be chased home from the train by ghostly canines or have to shake ectoplasmic poop from my shoe.

The real estate agent showed me the view, and the new linoleum in the kitchen, and emphasized that there was no credit check. She never mentioned that a sphinx lived next door.

My boyfriend wouldn't come with me to look at apartments. He's snobbishly opposed to anything beyond Manhattan, suspicious even that the world might really end at or above Eighty-Sixth Street. Gentrification was pricing Faery Folk out of Manhattan, and humans of a certain economic strata, namely me, were following. While the dark creatures that haunted Times Square sulked toward the further corners of the outer boroughs, and the magical beings that illuminated the East Village disappeared in the shadows of new luxury condos, people like my boyfriend moved in and claimed Manhattan safer, reborn.

I felt as if the city's very enchantment had lessened. I know he quietly feels that his rent-controlled apartment was something he had somehow *earned*, and the fact that I was forced to move due to rent increases was a personal tragedy, a fault of my own doing. I never mentioned that I could have just as easily moved in with him as moved to Brooklyn.

Actually I think Grecian sphinxes do have wings. He might have been right about that.

The cats in the hallway were great with mice and traditionally brought good luck—two residents won the lottery, big jackpots both. But the cats were also crafty and willfully rushed into your apartment the moment you cracked the door open. Then you had to feed them and pay their veterinary bills. Not a bad trade-off, assuming you could afford the vet bills, but if one of the cats lives with you, its face begins to take on your characteristics. A mute animal mirror of yourself always looking up at you, following you from room to room with a plaintive meow was disquieting, to say the least.

I went back to the refrigerator and rummaged for a can of beer left over from my housewarming party. I normally don't like beer, but I needed something to erase the acidic taste the wine had left in my mouth. I took a swig and thought about calling my boyfriend. He would try to get me to come over. He would dismiss my concerns and start talking about his co-workers. I gulped down the beer and went back to the peephole.

Why didn't I just ask him if I could move in with him?

The hall was tranquil, vacant; so I stepped out.

I bent down to leave the package at the Sphinx's door and smelled an allure of incense. It was a dry aroma, a spicy musk. Involuntarily, my eyes closed as I inhaled deeply. The door opened.

The Sphinx stood in the door frame, massive yet strangely lissome. Her golden fur shimmered like a distant desert mirage. I blinked and slowly picked up the package to present it to her. She slid back on spectacular brass claws, silently inviting *entrée*.

Overwhelmed, I obeyed.

The door closed. Her scent strengthened its hold on me. Cats twisted at her claws and eyed me with intolerance. Their faces were less human than the hallway cats, more imperial.

The arid scent burned with the rich smells of a summer afternoon; an overpowering curiosity arose within me like the wavering hallucinatory heat off a dangerous highway.

I followed her to the living room. The floor was bare; there was no carpet. As she padded before me I could tell that her claws never actually touched the wood; leathery heels elevated the Sphinx and kicked up airy tufts of cat fur. The television was on without sound. A game show. A spinning wheel. Expectant faces.

Commercial.

She turned.

Her voice was a strong whisper. The sound evoked ancient memories of shifting desert sands and vistas of monuments crumbling under a permanent boil of sun. "Open the package."

The beer felt heavy and sour in my stomach. I had the sudden, overwhelming need to urinate, to flee to my own apartment and lock the door. But I slavishly complied. I tore into the package at its damp spot. Wrapping paper fell to the floor in shreds. Cats nosed the curling shards with hungry suspicion.

My fingers were now sticky as I opened the cardboard box. It held two incredibly large cherries; corpulent twins effuse with an over-abundance of mysterious sweetness hung from a single thick black stem. Each cherry swirled a volcanic red.

The television flickered. Cats momentarily cocked their alien heads.

With effort, I tugged one of the heavy orbs from their uncompromising stem. It finally gave and I knowingly held out the cherry on my palm for the Sphinx to eat. I trembled as her philosophical tongue slid across my flesh. Her leonine face was an enigmatic canvas of perfect disdain. Casually working her jaw, she spat out the pit as I placed the other cherry between my teeth and pulled the stem. As I bit down, a fiery bile rose in my throat, and I accidentally swallowed the fruit whole.

My throat narrowed in anguish as I choked. The Sphinx slowly spread darkly angelic wings that had lain unnoticed, concealed within the folds of her pelt. She reached for the remote and turned up the volume.

A commercial ended. There was a burst of invisible crowd noise. Then expectant faces.

YOLK

Masa woke naked, floating in an egg. He had not shrunk. Rather the egg was large, big enough to contain him, allowing him to stretch and drift, content and warm. Too sudden a movement, however, and he would brush up against the shell. Not that it was a *very* large egg. Still it was more comfortable than confining. Immediately he sensed that he was inside an egg because he was embracing a large, wholesome yolk, the way your typical sleeper might hug a favorite pillow. The yolk was centrifugal, and Masa happy to hold on, feet out as the surrounding current of viscous albumen flossed his toes, cupping his muscular calves. The yolk glowed a soft yellow; an inviting amber. The enveloping egg-white swirled slowly and Masa felt as if the silk of the albumen were the milky rings of a planet; that he clung to a fragile world.

He let go of the yolk and slowly drifted. He painted the interior wall of the shell with his fingers; it seemed firm, with a rough consistency. And hard. This barrier would not be easily broken.

The glow of the yolk pulled him back. Knees up, he brought his fingers around the yolk to more fully embrace the mass. Warm egg-white knuckled his anus, the sensation spurred his erection. His bobbing cock lightly punctured the yolk; he felt electrified. He could see the shadowy curvature of his penis submerged in fluid gold -he'd always delighted in the uniquely sharp tip of his cock–the way the

39

tight foreskin bunched rather than retreated, giving a decidedly pointed, sword-like appearance to his already angular prick. The hair on his forearms wavered in the egg-white, looking to him like a giddy paramecium.

He dug his fingers into the yolk and it roiled. He pushed his forearms in deeper, up to his elbows. Within the confines of the shell a milky hurricane now unhurriedly churned. Phlegmatic shards spun off the central mass; a long tendril forced his lips apart to splice through the tiny gaps of his clenched, crooked teeth. The smear of egg-white that had lightly adhered to his eyes rippled, distorting his vision. This pressure intensified; he shut his eyes. Overwhelming darkness descended as the yolk, his center of gravity, dispersed; private universe in turmoil, his whole body clenched. Balled like an infant he ascended until, cupped by the cusp of the egg, he felt it tip and fall.

Masa woke in the bed of a stranger. The mattress was vast, a great plain. Bedposts rose like massive, black twisting tree trunks, their dark canopies joined far above. The high, miniscule points where the leaves interlaced shone the pinprick likeness of distant stars. Paisley sheets bunched and gathered, rolled like hills and valleys.

And there were tigers.

Black tiger, white tiger. Far off, eyeless beasts, giant cats that relied solely on a powerful sense of smell, roamed. Their joint roars crashed against the sheets. Masa cowered. He wore a tight tuxedo, high on his wrists and ankles.

A small flat fish clung to the ground like a footprint. It was a spiny flounder with poorly matched eyes fearfully searching the dry sky. Soon Masa noticed more of the fish sprinkled about; they were numerous, forming the paisley pattern that comprised the sheeted ground. These configurations were punctuated by weird, equally spiny shells, ancient mollusks and empty horns powdered with sand, their pink whorls pulsated with thirst. They were interspersed with black sand dollars. Shiny ebony discs caught the false starlight and flashed it back toward Masa.

The man with antlers stood high on a hill of fabric.

The man with antlers circled Masa while still keeping his distance. Masa kept an eye on him while peeling off the tuxedo. Naked, he felt free and buoyant, the giant mattress a sudden moonscape, littered with a school of fish beached in a teardrop mold. The folds of the sheets formed dry streambeds. Masa, arms out-stretched, ran down one such lane, care-free and smiling, the moon-breeze brushing his cheeks.

As he turned a bend in the stream, he surprised the man with antlers.

The man with antlers stood still, wary but curious, sniffing in Masa's direction with a wet, black nose. Tufts of brown, dirty hair sprouted from his shoulders. Otherwise he was nude, save a thick pelt which clung to his pelvis like moss. His skin was startlingly white. They circled each other. Masa noticed that the knuckles of the antlered man were red and cracked, as if he had recently been in a fight. They froze as twin tigers roared nearby. The man with antlers extended his hand. Masa took it and they sprinted down the dry streambed, away from the hungry howl of big cats.

They paused beside a bramble of driftwood bleached ghostly gray by inconsistent moonlight. They disentangled sweaty palms. Face to face, he examined his new friend's asymmetrical antlers. They rose from his temple like sturdy branches. Both were a gray ivory, darkened by multiple fissures. Each clutch possessed a different number of blunt points. Possibly some were broken off in forgotten duels. The man with antlers grinned. Masa smiled, too. Leaning in for a kiss, he was surprised by the cold wetness of the man's flat coal-button nose.

On his knees, Masa rested the palms of his hands on the boney ridges of the antlered man's feet. He delighted in the minute shifting of the man's toes, keeping time with the administrations of his tongue.

A nearby flounder, stapled to the ground by two corn-colored teeth, watched with wide, distraught eyes.

Masa woke up underground. Moist clumps of dirt hung from roots, dripping from a low yet unseen roof. It was hot in the cave. Fearful, Masa rushed forward, worried he would become mired in the soft dirt if he stood still, and that the loose dirt above would come crashing down. It was dark. He hit an earthen wall and pushed. It gave way.

Masa stumbled out, a slight avalanche spreading at his feet onto a grimy subway platform. This subway stop was still under construction. Lanterns hung from the low, still-earthen ceiling. Wheelbarrows of raw concrete were parked beside sharp pickaxes. The rumble of distant trains vibrated across the newly-tiled landing. A huddle of workers blocked the only exit of shiny metallic turnstiles, roped-off with yellow police tape.

The workers turned toward Masa. Big men slick with sweat, granules of dirt clung to their oiled bodies, massive shoulders pushing their torsos forward. Their small, mammalian faces were obscured by miner's helmets, each with a dim, cyclopean lamp. Large buckteeth buttoned lower lips. The Beaverhead closest to Masa approached. He had shovels for hands. His flattened fingers were fused together; his long, protruding thumbs wiggled constantly, as if proudly proving their independence. Masa stepped back. A train approached. Its horn sounded loudly. Masa peered down the tunnel. The train was actually a massive white worm, penile, eyeless and subterranean, inching forward on the force of its ribbed form. Masa sensed that the thing was endless. A huge lamp shone harshly out of its central drooling slit onto the freshly laid tracks. It struggled against the walls of the tunnel. Clumps of dirt fell from the ceiling. Beams buckled. The approaching Beaverhead plunged a shovel hand into Masa's chest. Masa reeled and stumbled back. More dirt fell. Masa turned, crying out in pain. He felt deeply stung. The Beaverhead had tried to pry loose his soul. The train-worm wailed as the tunnel collapsed in an endless roar of dirt. Masa dove toward the closing hole from which he had emerged.

He woke up inside Guillermo. Guillermo was his first lover at college. Neither of them spoke English well, nor did they understand a word of each other's native tongues. But they had smiled at one another on the soccer field, exchanged furtive glances in the dormitory showers. Now Masa was inside Guillermo, but not in the sense of their previous, rhythmic fusion. He was fully inside Guillermo, he wore his skin, filled his body with his own. Raising his hand he saw Guillermo's strong, stubby fingers, the bitten nails, the wide, honest palms. Masa sat up.

He was in Guillermo's bed, back at college in his lover's dorm. Sheets bunched at his feet. His boxers were twisted low on his waist, cracking the fly open, a thatch of Guillermo's bristly, ebony pubic hair rushed forth. Masa ran his fingers over his lover's chest, lingering at the polished copper pennies of his oval nipples. He felt Guillermo's cock stir and push against his boxers. Blood raced through the protruding veins of his forearms. His heart beat within Guillermo's heart, this double-engine fueled Guillermo's engorged cock. It rose steadily, meeting sweaty palm. He pressed the blunt fingertips of his other hand to his lover's dry, cracked lips. Their salty taste churned memories of surreptitious meetings after class. Thanksgiving, vacant hallways, their only uninterrupted weekend together. The first time either of them had seen snow. Masa's own erection filled Guillermo's like liquid metal. A shifting pink necklace of foreskin tightened as one erection threatened to push through the other. His lover's body unraveled as orgasm rose. Guillermo's chest split into ribbons and fell away as the first rivulet of semen pearled. Masa's thin, neat fingers scissored through his lovers hands. He felt his own true tongue wipe Guillermo's perfect, strong teeth.

His buttocks involuntarily tightened.

One leg jerked.

Cream startled his boxers with a milky pattern like the thick white folds of wax paper.

Masa woke up.

Suitcase Sam

Everyone called him Dio. He wasn't one to tell tales, though every old hustler has tales to tell. Not that anyone listens to the stories to begin with. That's the first thing you learn in a Times Square hustler bar, of which there are a diminishing few: everyone's talking, no one listens. The thing with Dio, he was different. He wasn't there to eke out a trick or scam drinks—he knew he was too old for that, he had too much dignity. Nor was he there to pay for it, either; the young Hispanic boys at the other end of the bar didn't interest him in the least. No, he was like me; he was here simply to drink, or pretend to drink while getting discreetly loaded in the bathroom.

Dio and I sized each other up early on and got along well. We were about the same age and of the same disposition, except I wasn't like Dio: I was buying, not selling, so the pseudo-macho boys at the other end of the bar were an occasional interest. But not so much. Like Dio, I liked to get loaded, though I was brazen enough that if I wanted to fuck one of them, we could do it in the bathroom; I didn't need to pay extra for a hotel room.

Dio would have still been cute if he hadn't turned so many tricks, or so studiously flirted with heroin. He looked used up. His features were good, but his skin was drawn in some places while slightly loose in others. He looked like cheap hotel furniture, worn but ready, durable. I guess we knew we could tell each other anything because we had done some bumps of smack in the bathroom stalls a few times. Anyone who snorts heroin instead of shooting thinks they're so fucking clever, beating the needle and all, like you can't get hooked: the kind of lie that makes for a natural friendship

So one night while we were particularly loaded, after many conversations, I confessed to Dio that I had once been married.

Nonplussed, he asked me *the* question. "Have you ever seen a Suitcase Sam?"

I didn't understand the question, was barely listening, in fact (we'd done some heavy bumps in the bathroom; everything glowed with that special, crinkly kind of yellow that shines through black and white movies as they age).

"No." I said. His forehead was shiny, with yellow spots. I thought I could detect the hidden grid of a car headlight.

He smiled and relaxed into his drink. A game of chess was on and he was in the lead. "That guy over there. He's a collector, that's what you call a guy who owns a Suitcase Sam. Most only own one. One's enough. But some guys, they've got to have everything."

I nodded, not knowing what he was talking about, but agreeing with the sentiment. I looked over at the guy. Typical of the older men who frequented an establishment such as this: perpetually on edge, probably married, a wedding ring heavy below the silt of change and lint in their pants pocket. Nurse one drink, score with the right hustler then off to a hotel that charges by the hour. "Funny thing about trade like that," Dio once told me, "all they want to do is suck cock. All this trade here, they're pussy bottoms, man." Except this guy who, ridiculously, wore sunglasses. He wasn't paying attention to the young men though, but conversed casually with the bartender. Otherwise he looked normal, a sad salesman, wide suitcase by his side a faded, pocked-plaid.

Dio said "Don't stare." So I looked away.

"So what's a Suitcase Sam?"

Dio took a long pull from his drink, dropped the tumbler so ice crashed against the glass, lit a cigarette and waited. I nodded to the bartender to fill his glass. As I had indicated earlier, he wasn't prone to histrionics or drama, so I figured this was worth my patience and money.

It was horrible, what he said.

We were so stoned, I guess it loosened more than his tongue, it cracked the safe where anyone would store such things that no one should know, and if you were privy to something of such a nature, would naturally lock away. Some things were never meant to be shared.

And no one shares their Suitcase Sam.

First Dio asked me if I'd ever heard of the slave auctions in the Meatpacking district. One night we had both laughingly confessed to having perused some the more tawdry bars in that locale. S&M shit. Though I had never been to such an auction I knew of them. It was no big deal–after all they advertise in the *Village Voice*. "Well, that's kindergarten. This is kindergarten, compared to a Suitcase Sam."

He measured me with a look that was disquieting, to say the least. And then the urge grew, just above my stomach. It always feels like that, when I'm ready for another bump, like someone opened a window inside me and the breeze blowing through might clean me out. I got up and went to the bathroom. Dio dutifully followed; as usual I was holding and he was not. Another bump. Then one for him, one for me. I collapsed lightly against the stall wall and slipped toward the floor, the porcelain bowl yawned slightly, the shreds of toilet paper floating within coalesced into a white, scarred tongue. I thought I could live there, right there on the dirty floor. Why do human beings need more space than this? This was perfect.

"So these Sams," he slurs. "They want this. They want to be owned."

He paused so I searched for something to say. I could hear an old man in the stall next to ours sucking a hustler's cock; I thought of animals gathering at a salt lick during the night near a cave:

carnivore rubbing shoulders with deer. A spring bubbling nearby. "Like a slave," I said.

Dio shook his head "no" for the longest time. I thought of how animal eyes captured in photographs taken at night have an added veneer; a blue florescent glow that erases the living pupil, creating saucers of cool pity.

"No no no," he said. "They want to be owned but they need, they need...the element of escape to be removed. A pet doesn't even know its property, it's so fully *owned.* " His eyes narrowed and focused at something over my shoulder, proud of his summation, as if it had only just occurred to him after years of searching. I looked at him, waiting for him to say more. I was comfortable leaning against the stall wall. Everything he had said was absorbed by the smack.

The ancient cocksucker next door slowed his slurping, the hustler, ready to burst, lit a cigarette. Smoke slowly poured over the partition. When you can hear someone giving head but can't see them, it sounds terribly like a child eating spaghetti. I wanted to share this stellar observation with Dio, but it seemed somewhat inappropriate, what with the topic at hand and all. I couldn't help smiling at my own thought though and he misinterpreted this as what, I don't know.

Dio got earnest. "See, they want to give up more then everything. I, I...everything's gone. The only thing left is inside and it can never get out." He shook his head as if overcome by a sadness that belied the effects of the smack I had generously just shared. Unexpectedly he pushed the stall door open and left.

Alone, I contemplated the sparkling toilet, mouth stretching in a huge "O"—as if about to draw breath. Next door I could hear the old man's soul flap its heavy vermillion butterfly wings as the hustler shot a load down his throat.

I didn't see Dio for a week after that.

Not that it bothered me. There are no expectations here. Scratch that. There's nothing but expectations but friendship just isn't one of them. Whenever Dio wasn't around I re-focused on the hustlers; ones I'd yet to sample. And I was patient. I wasn't interested in white poseurs flaunting ghetto chic; I like Hispanic and I like them young, tough. But every time I made a connection I thought of that old cocksucker that night in the stall beside me and imagined him on his knees, growing useless insect wings, tattered membranes weakly unfolding as he nurtured the youthful, thick cock in his mouth. I could see the boy's mulatto face; a slight mustache, bored expression, no hint of ecstasy. Invariably he would yawn and a mosquito's giant, gray proboscis would emerge to grease the old man's balding head.

So I was quietly relieved when Dio returned. And we did the dance, not greeting each other beyond a nod; I knew he was playing it cool. He didn't want to seem too eager to see if I was holding. Like I said, Dio had class.

Later in the night he saddled the stool next to mine and bought me a drink. Since he had last been in the bar the old man with the suitcase and sunglasses had yet to return–around midnight he came in, suitcase at his side. I said nothing.

Another thing about Dio, he drank scotch straight, as did I. All these hustlers, trying to look huge in their sweatpants, new sweatshirts unzipped low to reveal fine, broad, hairless chests overlaid with gold chains. All of them drank flamboyantly sweet drinks, sipping them noisily through the little stir straws.

Dio sighed and looked at me. He knew I remembered everything from our previous conversation, and that I was too much of a gentleman to demand an explanation.

"See, what I was talking about the other night, it should *never* be repeated." And he gave me a look that would crack tombstones. I nodded. "Okay. Listen. This is it. This is like the end of knowledge and what people will do. Do to each other." I felt cold but was desperate for him to continue. "See, a Suitcase Sam wants it, but they don't know what it is they want. It just happens to them when they run out of options. No more 'safe words,' no more dungeons and leather masks. This is something that cannot be bought or sold because slavery, for some people, is the greatest of freedom, a release from everything." He pulled himself away from his drink, squaring his shoulders as if he were ready for something to approach.

I downed my drink and tried not to stare at the old man. The suitcase sat at his feet. It was the same worn one as last time. It looked heavy. Full. The window above my stomach began to open again. Forgoing another drink I headed toward the bathroom. It was time for the first bump of the evening; Dio waited a few minutes before following me in.

In the stall I tapped out a tiny brown pinch on my wrist, inhaling deeply I closed my eyes. Luminescent larval cocoons spun about the room. Remembering my guest I opened my eyes and tapped out a graciously large bump onto his wrist. Dio inhaled, closed his eyes and waited. I listened to the room; a languid faucet dripped honey, no one else was here. So I grabbed onto my soul like a broomstick, aimed it a Dio and spoke oh-so deliberately: "Tell me."

He blinked, eyes sparkling, then delivered. "It's amazing. They carve a person down until they are the perfect...perfect *receptacle*." He nodded affirmatively as the smack raced through his veins. They carve people up until there is nothing left but the holes." He blinked. His eyes rolling behind his lids just a bit; I'd purposefully given him an extra large hit, wanting to get to the bottom of this.

Dio started a wet laugh. "See, cut off their arms and legs, blind them, pull out their teeth, and what do you got? Someone who lives in a suitcase, someone who aims to please because they can't aim at anything else."

Butterflies all around, invisible, threatening. I laughed, too. Preposterous. I poured out another two bumps each.

A minute later, "So you want to see a Sam." He wasn't asking. He knew my intentions.

"Sure."

"I can arrange it but you have to deliver. The old guy at the bar is hooked; he's been mainlining for over twenty years and if he's coming in here, he's running on empty. Meaning he'll do anything for a fix, even break the taboo and show us his Suitcase Sam." Dio looked at me. His eyes were glassy yet dry, like he hadn't cried in years.

The next night he arranged for us to see a Suitcase Sam.

And Dio was right: the old man was deep into his addiction and thus more prone to relax the strict code of secrecy among collectors. His apartment was nearby, in Hell's Kitchen. Ninth Avenue was a mess; a jumble of bars and dilapidated apartments, basically the spillover from Port Authority. We made our way up the dirty, uneven stairs of a five-floor walk up, knocked on the door then waited an inordinate amount of time. The old man answered the door, agitated.

Fat and gray, wrapped in an even grayer bathrobe, he let us in to an impossibly large apartment. An antique television broadcast indiscriminate images. I could see why he wore sunglasses at the bar; his eyes were fleshy, a pulpy maze of cataracts. He sat in the kitchen without saying a word, obviously waiting for a fix. Dio whispered to him assuredly while shooting me a rather serious look. I understood and produced a fresh bag of smack while Dio helped the old man secure his works. Grandpa was going to shoot his share of the dope, a procedure which always made me uncomfortable, so I looked away.

I studied as much of the place as I could in the dim light: a railroad apartment, every room tumbling into the other down scratched and dusty wooden floors; claw-like radiators gathered malevolently beneath each window. The old man got loaded, one arm tied off, slack skin hung lose beneath rubber tubing. His spoon fell to the floor. He sat in his chair, crusted eyes rolling back in his head.

"Let's take a peek." For the first time in our limited relationship, Dio sounded like a kid, excited, nervous. He led me to the front room, a dingy expanse overlooking Ninth, illuminated by the light of a long neon hotel sign.

Beside the bed sat a pregnant suitcase.

Dio used all of his strength to heft the bag up onto the sagging bed. He popped both locks. I urged him onward with my eyes. I was ready for a fix, a drink, for anything, anything but what was in that bag. Dio flipped the lid.

A torso but…not. An odd, puppet-like thing. But living. It moved. It was pared down to the minimum of what you could call human.

Vomit rose in my throat.

No legs, no arms, face disfigured, smoothed and limited. Sensing that its case had been opened it roiled; all oiled hairless muscle; greasy ball-bearings of flesh. Open toothless mouth pouring out an indefinable pain. Eyes removed, lids sewn shut in a neat series of X's; ears soldered closed, everything shaved: the scalp and chest hairless. Buttocks pulsating, cheeks clapping like a trained seal ready for a treat. Really, this was a thing, a thing with two gruesome mouths; its anus distended from obvious, repetitious abuse, pummeled into a purple pout, greedy lips, sick mimic to the soundless pucker at the other end. Just then it whinnied. The strange noise rattled from within its chest, guttural.

I couldn't help but take a closer look. Its tongue had been sheared as well. Arms clipped neatly at the shoulder, the legs taken as close to the pelvis as possible, all sealed with a thick scar of gristle. Moving like a desperate snake unable to shed a burning skin, frenzied from the attention, its genitals were gone, nothing but a mass of red scar.

Dio stood back, proud, responsible. "That's a Suitcase Sam.

"We might as well feed it." And he unzipped his pants and pulled out his cock, squat and limp but rising. The Suitcase Sam wagged in anticipation. He fed his thickening member into the red raw mouth. It hummed with delight, gumming and slurping at Dio's dick while still in its luggage bassinette. I didn't want to see this so I turned and took a desperate bump off my wrist.

Back at the bar Dio was all talk. He was like a fountain -having finally found a confessor. Though I was more dazed than truly dedicated to such travesty, I had to know.

"I found out about them from a guy I know who deals Ketamine, he gets it off a veterinarian who does the procedures. They're a tight group. Tighter than the snuff flicks crew but definitely a scene that likes to get together. These collectors, they *show*. Like fucking dog shows. And they take them with them *everywhere*. It's a whole culture."

He spilled the whole story. How they had been around for years. They were the last stop in the sexual underground. Total domination meets surgical submission, taking slaves from auctions and other masters and *diminishing* them; paring them down to base elemental attributes. Fed cock and baby formula, they were clean-shaven to augment the fact that they were ornament, not person. Most were smallish men, chosen for their thin, compact torsos. Apparently their life-span isn't terribly long. It's easy to forget to feed something habitually left in a suitcase—a real problem collector's lament.

Dio told a funny story about a collector who purposely carried his bag at the airport. When it was scanned the baggage checkers naturally inquired. The collector coolly replied that he was transporting an anatomical dummy and nothing more. No one checked. I mean, why would they?

I felt uneasy that Dio was telling me so much at the very place where we had first seen a collector, there at the other end of the bar, as if this place was *theirs,* our conversation a knowable violation. I wanted to go somewhere else, but didn't want to interrupt his story, it was too unreal. I had jut seen the world on a leash. Dio had inadvertently stumbled onto a secret that was the prelude to real danger. The pouch of smack in my breast pocket felt like bubblegum.

This bar, my thoughts, Dio's conversation, even my clothes, everything felt extremely claustrophobic. "Look. I've got to go." I pushed away from the bar and fled. I don't think Dio noticed I had left in a panic; we were too loaded to touch our drinks but he was staring into the slope of ice and liquor in his half-lifted glass. Dio was frozen in the moment, as if the wave building enough strength

to crush him had also lifted him far enough aloft until he could see
the ocean in its entirety.

I entertained the idea of not going back to the bar, of doing
something else, maybe checkout one of the clubs in the Meat Packing
District. But they didn't open until late. I didn't want to score but I
did. Restless, I got on the train and went downtown. At the bar Dio
was talking quietly to Randy, a young hustler new to the bar, new to
the game. He had a quick smile, the largest, whitest teeth you had ever
seen and massive, black biceps highlighted by a new, white sleeveless
t-shirt. No doubt Dio was dispensing tips of the trade, so I sat on the
periphery. Then I noticed Dio had a suitcase tucked between his legs.
I froze and thought about getting up, but Randy was eyeing me so I
returned the smile. He must have been thirsty, hoping I would buy
him a drink. I pulled out a twenty and told him to play a song in the
jukebox. He got the hint and took off. The bartender brought me a
drink and I turned to Dio. "Taking a vacation?"

He laughed and patted me on the shoulder. "I'm going to take you
for the ride of your life, my friend. Want to go to a convention?"

I eyed the bag at his feet. It lacked the radioactivity of the old
man's luggage from the previous night. "What's up?"

"If you give the old man a gram, we're in. We just walk in with
him and no trouble. It just so happens that there's a convention in
town tonight. This bag is just cover. We won't go in until everyone
else is there. No one will notice that we didn't open ours." He patted
the bag at his feet.

The window above my stomach opened wide. I felt ready to dive
in so I got up and went to the bathroom. Dio waited a few minutes
and then followed me in.

We did a whole night's worth back at the bar, so to re-supply
and score for the old man we had to go back to my apartment. Dio
whistled appreciatively as I opened the door. I explained to him

that the place isn't really mine. I rent it from an old college friend; it's been in his family for years so its rent stabilized–meaning I pay a ridiculously low amount, probably what keeps me in drugs. All of the furniture is theirs. I own nothing but my clothes and a few unread books.

I called my guy. My dealer only makes house calls. That's how the best ones do it. Dio sat there nervously, rubbing his hands on his thighs while I eyed the suitcase. I gave it a lift: light as a feather. I went out on the balcony and grabbed a loose brick from under a barren flower pot. I wrapped it in a towel and placed it in the suitcase. Hefting the bag, Dio smiled as my door buzzer rang.

The trip downtown was a marvelous rollercoaster ride, skyscrapers bent like palm trees in our wake, the neon signs of Times Square celestial gates to somewhere *delicious*. The old man wouldn't get in the cab until he scored so we went upstairs and waited for him to shoot. We did some bumps. He shot again then we were out. I noticed that his suitcase was identical to ours, resting side-by-side between him and Dio. I was paranoid that they would accidentally switch them; I couldn't stop imagining scenarios where this indeed happened, costing us our precious lives: being caught and fed to a kiddy-pool filled with Suitcase Sam's fitted with sharp silvery dentures, blindly snapping away. Or the old man, opening his suitcase and the brick and towel falling out; shrugging and pointing to us and the collectors standing impatiently as doors swing open and huge men in medical gowns and surgical masks lead Dio and I away. I recognize one of the men behind his mask. It's Randy from the bar. He flashes me a huge smile, stretching his mask until the cotton almost rips. My fear solidified when I realized we were driving over the Manhattan Bridge—I didn't know we were leaving the city.

Driving through Brooklyn, I was mesmerized by the dark landscapethe low buildings and weak streetlights, shuttered store fronts and weedy vacant lots, the occasional burning shopping cart. We were back on an expressway then off again, idling in front of a non-descript hotel; a plane roared by overhead, the sign over the building across the street was in Korean. We were near JFK.

We got out of the cab and followed the old man through the hotel lobby. No one was behind the desk. I renewed my fear of the switched suitcases and stared hard at both of them, then lit a cigarette. The old man pushed through unguarded double-doors and into a non-descript banquet hall. All of the tables were pushed against the wall so that the room was ringed with chairs, many of them vacant, others occupied by empty suitcases. I was glad I lit the cigarette; it gave me a focus, something to pull my attention, however briefly, away from the horror on the floor.

At first the room looked like it was filled with proud parents, milling about as their babies frolicked on the floor. My initial thought was of infants, their floundering movements and hairless heads. No, the heads were too large, and only the ones on their backs floundered about; any Suitcase Sam upright scrambled oddly fast, raised slightly on their nubs, sideways like a crab. Very fast, one came at me, red open mouth a vacuum-like wound. A large, gregarious-looking man in a weathered cowboy hat broke away from his group and followed quickly behind the creature, scooping it up as I lifted my leg in revulsion. "Ups-a-daisy there, Beatrice! Sorry partner, she sure gets excited when she's around new people."

She. Dio said that all of the collectors referred to their Sam's as "she." The thing smacked its toothless jaws at me; strained movement behind the angry X's where eyes should be. The man asked me where I was from.

"The Upper Eastside." *What's next? Is he going to ask me what I majored in at college?*

"Great city you all got here. Hope to take in a show this trip." He placed Beatrice on the floor, faced it toward a pile of Suitcase Sam's bumping and nibbling on each other in the middle of the room, then sauntering away with a wave of his hand behind his head. Men were clustered about the room. A few huge, bearish men in leather kept their Suitcase Sams on shiny leashes, in matching miniature leather attire. Most were dressed casually and talked seriously, arms-crossed, about the care of their Suitcase Sam.

"Don't shave hon, wax." "If I'm at work I keep him in diapers –everyone but me has a Sam that can go on newspaper." "This is my second Sam. I brought both to the San Diego Con but they fight, so I only travel with one."

Sams scampered across the floor. Beatrice circled a yawning, pinkish Sam, a ball of taut muscle–as if removed limbs and curtailed senses had somehow refocused its energy into a glistening torso mad with veins and overly-accentuated arteries. The thing's shaved eyebrows had been replaced by long-healed symmetrical scars of meticulously placed cigarette burns. Human topiary. A bland woman with glasses and unnecessarily long, straight hair hefted her Sam in her arms like a massive infant while listening to whatever advice the twin leather daddies dispensed, their legs slowly entwined by their be-leashed pets.

Somehow I had failed to notice that Dio and the old man had crossed the room. I didn't think I could walk across such a minefield; a landscape of moving flesh and indifferent collectors. I could see smudged chalk out-lines on the carpet. There must have been a race earlier. With prizes, I bet.

The old man was opening his suitcase. My heart, already sluggish from the smack, lurched into action. I remembered the possibility of switched bags. I wanted to cross the room but my feet were heavy, the carpet a muddy river, Suitcase Sams surfacing, faceless prehistoric turtles mad to gum my ankles. Well, I thought, if it's okay to smoke in here maybe I could to do a discreet bump; I needed something to help me cross *that* room. The old man hoisted his Sam from his case. It bleated in pleasure as he held it above his head in a surprising show of strength and pride. Dio nodded and smiled and placed his unopened case down beside the old man's. Relieved, I walked slowly to the closest seat, sat down and felt at the deflated bag in my shirt pocket. It was flat, empty. We'd started too early and shared the last batch with the old man in its entirety. I thought about finding the bathroom and splitting the bag open; there had to be half a bump of dust in there at the least. I would need to be in my apartment to call my dealer and he wouldn't like coming up there twice in one night. Dio sat down next to me.

"Interesting party." He patted my leg, removing his hand to reveal a fat bag of smack.

More than a gram.

Surprised, I asked "Where did you get this?"

Dio feigned a hurt look. "I owe you."

"Is it okay if I do a bump here?" I covered the bag with the small of my hand. The corners of the plastic bag cut into it like a budding diamond.

"Look around. You think anyone is going to call the cops?"

The old man had come to life in the middle of the banquet room, slapping backs and vigorously shaking hands. Dio rocked back in his chair.

I tapped out a bump of his stuff on my wrist and took a deep hit. Looking at the bag I noticed his shit was darker than what I usually score, grainer, too. And it hit me like a shotgun blast. Powder burns darkened the edges of my perception. Brown shadows expanded, seeping out from behind the vending machine in the corner, the folded chairs by the door. And then everything got brighter.

A Suitcase Sam bumped my feet.

Beatrice again, beautiful. In my earlier panic I hadn't noticed the skillful tattooing which adorned her flesh. She was lightly covered with the mocking imprimatur of a famous Italian luggage design, replete with a floppy handle sewn into the small of her back. She sucked at the corner of my shoe as the shadows darkened. I looked longingly at the door. I saw the gray shape of the cowboy approaching, arms extended. Then I blacked out.

⚭

I woke up with a start violent enough to knock over the chair beside me. I had trouble opening my eyes and this instantly filled me with dread. Nearly hyperventilating, not knowing where I was, I felt for my wallet. It was there. I noticed my shoes were off. Rubbing sleep from my eyes, I looked around: I was still in the banquet hall. The place was empty. Breathing deeply, the air stale from old cigarette smoke, I tried to stand, thought better of it and sat back down.

The bellmen ignored me as I left the hotel. Likely I was an unwanted reminder of something they were paid triple to ignore. I stumbled out into the parking lot. Receding daylight: I wasn't just asleep, I must have been unconscious. I didn't have enough money for a cab; the rocking assurance of the A train would help clear my head.

On the train my mouth was dry. My head felt cleaved, as if I'd been hit by an ax, wound invisible.

At the Franklin Avenue stop a gaggle of old women boarded the train, matching outfits and bowling bags, heading into the city for a night out. One old lady rested her white, withered hands across a pert, zippered bowling bag, gossiping close with her compatriot. I stared at the bag. Round, petulant, I heard it whisper. Velvety voices from within the other bags joined in. A barely perceptible chorus arose, masked by the machine-hiss of train making track.

Next stop, Hoyt Street, I got off.

CROYAL CATAMITE

Losing my arms felt natural, like shuffling off dead skin. I do most things with my mouth anyway. If need to I can open doors. With minor discomfort I could turn a door's handle with my mouth. The next person who wishes to enter the room may recoil at the damp handle, but I've made my entrance and exits in life with regard to no one. Since losing my arms I prefer not to stand. My sisters joke that I've spent most of my short life on my knees anyway, so I should find it quite natural. The act of standing requires too much balance, so I recline most of the day. I walk only when necessary. Someone is always near to prepare my opium and light my pipe.

I did not have my arms buried. The idea was too morbid for me to entertain. They were burned by the gardeners of the court, raked into the refuse of the kitchen. The Assistant Sub-Chamberlain, as fussy as all eunuchs, had a burial site prepared the minute he learned I had ceded the unnecessary ligaments, but I saw through his charitable efficiency; to have a portion of myself buried was to further shorten the link between death and myself. He would have pieces of me in storage for whatever spell he may wish to cast in some unfathomable future plot. I refused and when he left sent for the gardeners. As the Emperor's Catamite I receive no respect, but I *am* obeyed.

The Emperor, being Emperor, did not even notice I was without arms. My unique supplication before him does not require the use of a single finger. I expected no remark and would have dreaded any utterance other than the concise praise he occasionally expresses as I complete my task. An observation on the part of the Emperor would mean my services no longer held the singular, hypnotic sway which elevated (lowered, my sly sisters would correct) my position in life. His Highness strokes my hair while I work him in my mouth.

My father taught me the thirty-three techniques of pleasure within our discipline when I lost my front teeth. At that youthful age catamites are prized possessions among wealthy merchants and senior monks and I was to be auctioned off the moment I had mastered the appropriate methods of oral pleasure. Thankfully my father recognized talent and I was not sold. After lending me to his favorite brothers, he and my uncles agreed I was indeed gifted. Though I was not a particularly remarkable purveyor of the ancient techniques, when I opened my mouth an uncanny, enchanting sense of surrender issued forth, which, my uncles all commented, made me feel as if I were a necessary appendage to their cocks, a mouth born uniquely to them and them alone. I was a lock that shrunk or expanded to their individual keys. My family recognized the value of such a treasure and allowed my adult teeth to emerge, shortened and rounded, ever so slightly, by a minute amount of filing. Nor was I castrated on my thirteenth birthday. I was not to be made a common eunuch. I was groomed for royal service. At thirteen I was prostituted out at an exorbitant fee. This insured a magnitude of curiosity and a minimum of customers; only the richest would act on their curiosity and I would not be overly used by the time word of my powers reached the Emperor.

The Emperor had recently ascended the throne and was only a few years my senior. The Royal Mother was acting regent. She had rid our empire of her tyrannical husband and though relieved, the world watched wearily as this new monarch matured. We rejoiced as signs of benevolence and wisdom graced his initial rule. Soon I was sent for.

My father brought me from our village to the palace, and for once father rowed us up the Yangtze River himself; he did not want me overtaxed upon my presentation to the Emperor. At night water snakes menaced our boat and would strike futilely at the bow. The monkeys in trees applauded and laughed at our trip. I could smell the city before I saw it: shit and incense. Occasionally father would use his pole to push away a corpse that would bump our skiff like a tender log. I asked him why bodies always floated face down. He said it was because they were embarrassed to be poor and unburied.

I was brought before the Emperor in a simple, private ceremony after one of his sumptuous banquets. Led in by the Chamberlain himself I knelt on a silk pillow embroidered with soft gold, mouth open. I knelt there in complete surrender, much like the entire world the Queen Mother had placed at His Excellency's feet. The only difference being that, given the chance, I would not bite. With His virginity insured for the arranged marriage some months off, the Royal Catamite was a font of pleasure until His Highness wed and could accrue a harem. I quivered at the thought of the luxury and riches awaiting me if I were so chosen. The Emperor circled me the way a reluctant owner might assay a new horse, wary of being thrown. Eventually he lifted his robes and mounted my face. My jaw went slack, more so than was necessary for my uncles; my Lord was big but his thrusts were without experience but of willful energy. I had never had a youthful man and liked the newness of his musk, fermented from an afternoon on horseback, was of obvious royal vintage; the divine strength barreled in the hard belly pushing against my nose both humbled and excited me. This joy did not show, however. I am a professional. My tongue became his muscle. I knew for his every thrust when to parry, when to suck. He emptied voluptuous milk into my mouth, which I had been coached to spit into the cloth proffered by the Assistant Sub-Chamberlain. This fluid was rushed to the Royal Falconry where it is fed to His Highness' favored hunting birds, forming a powerful bond between Emperor and Falcon.

It is forbidden to swallow the Royal fluid. It drives Empresses mad, poisons lowly catamites like myself. The Emperor offered me a slight pat on the head. The Chamberlain tugged on the back of my collar and I was removed from the room. The young Emperor had approved; my future was assured.

That night I was not returned to my father's care. I was given a large suite of rooms near the Emperor's quarters; my father was paid a huge sum while soldiers fetched my sisters. Thus my father was doubly blessed with a bag of gold while his household was relieved of three burdensome dowries.

Younger than even I, I fear palace life has spoiled my sisters. They quickly learned the court dialect and gossip like witches, tease the Assistant Sub-Chamberlain charged with our care, and generally cause enough mischief among the palace staff to bring unwarranted attention on my choice, most private office. I love them dearly. Little Sister combs my long, dark lifeless hair every night. Big Sister braids. Young Sister holds my mirror for me while Little Sister draws the bath. I bring them all into the hot waters with me and we laugh and chase bubbles among the floating perfumed petals until the black water cools. Our bath is larger than the house in which we were raised. The furniture is luxurious, fine, exact replicas of the Emperor's drawing room. Should he ever have the desire to take me in my own quarters, everything is as he should find it in his own room. He has never visited me in my own quarters, which is fine—I prefer to go to him. The ritual of crossing the hall readies me; I feel as if I am being pulled by an invisible fishing line tied to my tongue, reeled by his impatient, wagging pole. He never meets my mouth soft. At first I considered this a sign of his youthfulness, but now that he is married, I know it is a sign of appreciation. As the burdens of kingship weigh on him more and more, I, and I alone, can alleviate that weight. He rises when I enter, robe open, cock buoyed on certain ecstasy. Dependant solely upon me.

Historically, among Royal Catamites, only I have performed my services eyes open. This initially caused consternation among the Chamberlain, the Assistant Sub-Chamberlain, and various staff, as no one is to view His Highness in the throes of ecstasy. I was dully warned to keep my eyes closed.

Why are your eyes, then, open? I countered.

We gaze down at the floor at all times, Catamite. Down, that is, toward you. The Assistant Sub-Chamberlain angrily replied.

The Chamberlain himself, so used to addressing Royalty, never deigned talk to me. This answer did not faze me, nor did I change my habit. Early on I realized that my role fell under the exclusive provenance of the Emperor. I keep my eyes open but unfixed. I offer mirrors, not approbation or appreciation. I am a conduit and nothing more.

So well adapted to his needs, I have become indispensable. The Emperor, in his youthfulness, uses me several times a day, making my sisters a swirl of activity, keeping fresh silk robes ready, steeping green tea always on hand to revive me. I know of the other catamites he purchased, but they wither (for lack of a vine) on their dusty divans. I refuse their company. The Emperor takes me most afternoons and nearly every night. Positions change as well. In the evening he prefers to recline. I cling to him until his seed in its entirety fills my mouth. The Assistant Sub-Chamberlain is no longer required to empty my mouth for me; I spit out his treasure into the golden cloth to pass the Assistant Sub-Chamberlain after my exit. Even in marriage, the young Empress (the Empress!) is dismissed so I can dutifully perform my task. Occasionally he looks into my eyes. I refuse to focus. When he looks into me I do not want him to see fear or love, only his own power. His eyes, though, are often closed. My tongue swabs the head of his cock in lubricating saliva during the initial kiss; on being summoned I cease to swallow, to better provide His Highness with the immediate bath of my willing orifice.

I never take his considerable length entirely into my mouth upon arrival. That action keeps until my Lord is closer to climax. To better give him a sense of completion, that my use has reached conclusion, only then do I take him to the root and his pleasure issues forth.

I enjoy my quarters and have no complaints. Over these many months, however, I secretly began to feel his pleasure should be mine as well. A catamite knows not to pleasure himself while providing service, indeed, not to even experience arousal. *Fine, but what of afterwards*? I am a servant. But how could I sup for so long only to feel starved? I wanted to keep his pleasure inside me. No longer satisfied with being the lock, I wanted to be the actual treasure chest as well. The opportunity had come once before, had taken me by such surprise I did not know it was to my benefit. One night, before dismissing me, and much to my astonishment, the Emperor used me twice. Before his youth passed or his passions turned toward his growing harem, I would make use of this situation. I did not have to wait long. One night, as I withdrew and deposited his fluid into the golden cloth, the Emperor kept his hand on my braid, playfully coiling it around his strong palm, drawing me back to his rising cock. This was my chance. I slowly lowered my open mouth, using my tongue as a guide I went to the root and he gasped. With newfound precision, I turned my head to engulf his strength and methodically pumped him back to full size. He bucked; my braid now wrapped tightly in his hand, to better control my movement. I felt release mounting within him and was ready.

I swallowed the heat in my mouth. Swallowed? I deliriously *coveted*.

Task complete, I rose and left the Emperor's chambers. Spent, he was asleep across his bed before the door closed. I carelessly tossed the gold cloth, full from our previous encounter, toward the Assistant Sub-Chamberlain, who leapt to catch it as if it were a fragile gem that would burst upon hitting the floor. Well, he *is* a eunuch. What would he know of such matters?

I was not exhausted but elated. The membranous cream in my mouth slid slowly down my throat, luxuriantly downward, lining my stomach with Royal yolk. I felt as if a heavenly blacksmith had lifted me by the heel to dunk me in a warm, frothy potion, giving me a visible coat of milky gold. And the promise of immortality. My sisters offered me a relaxing bath and I refused, choosing, instead, to recline on my favorite divan, alone, savoring the thickness which coated my tongue: I had eaten the rarest delicacy on earth, the wet spark around which the world turns.

Later, relenting to my increasingly concerned sisters, I took my bath. Darkly, I sank up to my chin, worried if the rumors of death and madness were true. I refused to let superstition ruin my coup. That night I slept as if on clouds, elevated on the very breath of powerful dragons!

A few weeks later a slight itch commenced at my shoulders. My arms felt tired. It was easier to call Little Sister to peel my fruit or light my pipe than to do it myself so I wasn't much concerned. Still, the ever-observant Assistant Sub-Chamberlain summoned the Royal Physician. Without examination, he sent unguents and creams. Young Sister dutifully applied these as Little Sister and Big Sister plied court intrigue from the Royal Physician's sheepish page. The irritation and lethargy increased, spreading, ever so slightly, to my legs. One evening in the bath my toenails slid off, little brown rafts floating across the bubbles. This time the Royal Physician came. He questioned my activities. He asked if I partook in the Royal fluid. I looked at him with all of the anger I could pretend to muster yet remained silent. The Assistant Sub-Chamberlain stepped forward to volunteer that he had received the appropriate deposit each and every time my use had been required by His Highness. This was done less in my favor and more to assure that his assignment was consistently and correctly completed.

The physician and Assistant Sub-Chamberlain talked amongst themselves. I overheard the Physician whisper that he supposed some amount of Royal fluid would seep into my bile, but not enough to cause concern. They agreed that the Emperor should not be told. It was imperative to the Empire that His Highness was well served. I was to continue my duties until the Royal Physician could further assess my condition.

A week later, due to an unrelated matter, the Royal Physician was beheaded, along with half the court. When word reached us the Assistant Sub-Chamberlain looked at me, I at him, as Little Sister combed my hair, Big Sister patiently waited to braid. That night, in what I assume was a fitful sleep, my arms fell off. I awoke feeling, not panic, but simply, inexplicably, lighter. There was no pain. Standing felt alien, as if I had been spun blindfolded and then told to walk a straight line. I laughed at this novelty and my sisters, rushing in, commenced to cry at the wilted limbs lying at the foot of my tousled bed. I calmed them. I told them that the Emperor had told me to rid myself of my limbs as they were unnecessary to my task. I scolded them. *Really, what need have I of hands with three busy sisters to keep after me? Why, if I were good with my hands would I even need you here? Now get busy, Little Sister, prepare my morning meal! Big Sister, I'm cold without my robe!*

They shed suspicious tears but eventually their sorrow faded and they happily went about preparing for the day.

I continue serving the Emperor. I am a funnel of consistency. However, of late my knees have begun to itch more and more. And my knees are my fulcrum. Without legs the Emperor might find my appearance too disturbing to keep me. Surely the now slight tail growing from my backside points toward my imminent destruction. I know what has brought about my transformation, and, ultimately, will deliver my end. The Emperor, too, will soon know when my tiny fangs, pulsing with milky gold venom, more fully emerge.

MISHIMA DEATH CULT

fter doing a few lines of Ritalin off the cover of his Social Studies textbook Kyle forgets what video game he is playing and stares blankly at the screen. The pixel bodies of the electric combatants flicker in unison to his rapid blinking. Kyle thinks maybe his blinking controls the flickering image so he stops and stares hard at the glowing marionette ninjas. Sure enough, their flickering stops. High on his psychic mastery of the universe, he leans back onto the carpet, lifting his T-shirt to wipe his nose—a trail of snot glittery with granules of chopped-up Ritalin streaks across his black shirt. Looking up at the ceiling fan he tries to stop the blades from turning. No luck. He must have used all his powers on the video game. The CD changer clicks and whirls. Death metal rattles out of the speakers; he can't remember what was playing before. He fingers the Tarot cards strewn across the deep blue carpet. The cell phone he found at the Cinnabon at the mall rings, but he ignores it. Rachel stirs on the bed, though. All he can see is the straw of her black hair poking out above the folds of his comforter.

Kyle stares at the fan until the blades stop, stop, hesitate then spin in reverse.

The cell phone rings again. This time Kyle answers it.

"You stole this."

"I found it."

Pause.

"Give it back." Kyle hears a chewing sound. Gum. Or carrots. He can't tell if the young voice belongs to a boy or a girl.

"Suck my dick." Kyle grins into the fan.

Pause.

"Uh."

Pause.

"Okay. Where do you live?"

"Miramar." Kyle rubs his crotch.

Pause.

"Too far." Click.

Kyle stares at the phone. A Nokia. "Big deal," he says, and throws it into the lap of the beanbag across the room. He wonders about the voice on the other end, though. Definitely young. Possibly another recruit. Kyle has started a cult and needs recruits. You just can't burn down a school or have a decent massacre with only four kids. Kyle wants a dozen. *Needs* a dozen.

Rachel wants to go to the mall to see the new *Hellraiser* film. They climb up on his roof to smoke a joint before she leaves. Kyle wonders if he were to kill her and leave her on the roof, would his parents smell the body? He coughs out a really deep hit and asks her opinion.

She holds her hit of pot in for as long as possible "Heat rises." They stare at the sky for awhile. A plane moves across the sky. "So, how would you kill me?"

"I'd choke you, of course." Kyle replies. He stares at the empty sky. He's been up on the roof enough times to know another jet will appear in exactly five minutes. Rachel reapplies black lipstick, works her bra and says "Promises, promises."

She fishes for the ladder with the heel of her pump, goes over the edge and is gone. Another jet slips by above.

⌒

Back in his room Kyle calls Randolph from the cell phone. He tells him that there will be a meeting tonight at his house and that everyone should wear black. In anticipation of the meeting Kyle unfolds a large square Japanese flag and tacks it to the wall above his stereo and television. He hopes the creases fall out before everyone shows up. He can't ask his mom to iron the flag as she'll ask a *billion* questions. At their meetings, they watch one of the Faces of Death sequels then discuss their plans to destroy the school. Not tonight. Kyle wants things to move forward, and this means coming up with a manifesto and discussing recruitment. He knows Rachel only comes because she's bored and in love with him. Randolph comes because he doesn't have any friends and is in love with him, too. That's okay. Kyle doesn't believe in love. Only guys are allowed to spend the night, so on weekends Randolph sleeps over and sucks his dick. He's been stoned enough to suck Randolph's tiny dick a few times. The boy's eyes rolled back, and his tongue shot out like a cuckoo clock. Blowing Randolph is like sucking a little boneless thumb. Big Deal.

He doesn't swallow but Randolph does. He saves the Kleenex from when he masturbates and hands them to Randolph when they pass in the hall at school. Randolph blushes and shoves them into his pockets and he *believes*. Kyle knows he believes. Randolph will do whatever he tells him to do in the name of the cult, but only because he loves Kyle. Daisy, however, loves the cult. Kyle is impressed by her devotion. Disturbed as well. She reads too much. For Kyle there was some serious trepidation in starting a cult over a literary figure, but he thought he could handle it. After all, a cult is supposed to be a religion, and his only religious experience in his entire life happened while watching a movie about Mishima.

He smoked three or four joints with Rachel that night before settling into the nest of his bed as the film filled his room with that particular blue of television's second-hand light. Halfway through the movie he looked at her to see if she was *getting it* and she was;

she was equally entranced. When the movie ended he was more than *wowed*, he was *ready*. The next day at Barnes & Noble, Rachel and he held hands among the bookshelves. There were many books by Mishima. Kyle bought what he could afford. Together, they looked up Mishima on the Internet. The black-and-white photo of Mishima's severed head became the wallpaper on his computer, a pristine Dell his parents bought for him last Christmas.

He devoured *Confessions of a Mask,* read first because the title sounded like something Metallica would title an album. Having seen the movie millions of times now, he sees where Mishima was gay. He missed that before; *Confessions of a Mask surprised him. Kyle* gave his copy to Randolph because he knew Randolph was gay. Everyone in school knows Randolph is gay. Randolph seems ready to shrink: messy blond hair melds into a pale complexion made paler by his choice of dark, dark, loose fitting clothes. Goth band T-shirts so large they hang off the bullet of his neck and shoulders like a sack.

That following Monday after he saw the movie Kyle couldn't stop talking about Mishima. About how much he *cared*. Cared enough to die for something he believed in. How he was really, really the Kurt Cobain of Japan. *But cooler*–Mishima tried to overthrow the government. If Cobain had walked on stage and started pumping a shotgun into the audience, well, he would have been a God. Kyle didn't realize he was shouting this to Rachel on the bleachers as they sat out gym class. Sometimes he shouts when he doesn't mean to. Daisy, fat pimply Daisy, whom he never talked to but who always gravitated toward them–at a distance you'd think she were part of their group, someone one who had friends–Daisy listened to every word Kyle said and went to the school library and checked out one of Mishima's books. She read the whole novel that night then returned to school the next day and checked out another. Daisy rented the movie. A week later she approached Kyle when he was alone in the hall and told him Mishima was a much better writer than either Anne Rice or Stephen King. Kyle just blinked at her, confused. He was half-way through *Confessions of a Mask*, and all he could think was: *Is this fat chick calling me a faggot? If Randolph told her about last Saturday night I'm going to step on his neck.*

Kyle stared at Daisy, fingering the foil-wrapped porcelain wafer of Ritalin in his pocket, when Daisy leaned in and whispered in his ear. *I've seen the movie twice now. Wouldn't it be great if somebody did something like that here?*

He pinched the pill in his pocket to dust, leaned into her ear and whispered back. *That's exactly what I'm planning. You're in.*

He walked away with no idea where that came from, barely any idea where it was going. He couldn't finish *Confessions of a Mask*, but read in two days the book his mother bought at the supermarket checkout about the Heaven's Gate Cult. Kyle then told Rachel and she kissed him. Kyle told Randolph and he nodded and said *Wow*. When he told Daisy that the first meeting would be after school at his house she took the folded Japanese flag out of her backpack and gave it to him. *Scary*, Kyle thought, making the mental note that when they massacre the school, to make sure her gun had blanks.

He's only half-troubled that Daisy's read a lot of Mishima's books—so far it's been more useful than anything, like she's doing homework for all of them or something. He's only read the one, or most of it, anyway. He's been careful though, to buy all of the books and to keep them in his room. One, *Sun and Steel*, he found used at the bookstore where he and Randolph buy comics. This book seems different from the others. For one thing it's hardback and actually has a photo of Mishima in a loincloth with a sword on the cover. He showed the book to the group and proudly claimed that that was the sword with which Mishima was beheaded, that he had read it on the internet. Randolph often cradled the book at meetings, like it contained their commandments.

Kyle found the book impossible to decipher. He would stare at the words and their cold poetry was lost on him, instructions to assemble something, the words marching around like fervent mechanical ants, never quite taking shape. Though *he* knew he and the cult were the parts to be assembled, he knew that much. The black and white photo of Mishima with sword showed a man with complete control. Every muscle was perfect and full. Kyle started doing push-ups every morning to Metallica's greatest CD, *Kill 'Em All*.

Daisy will occasionally mention a scene in a book that she thinks relevant and after the meeting Kyle will pour through that novel, searching for meaning. His particular coup was finding a copy of a film based on *The Temple of the Golden Pavilion*, checking out the Cliff's Notes to make sure the movie didn't deviate from the book–then casually quoting widely from the book, to impress the cult and keep Daisy from feeling superior. In the book a retarded monk burns an important temple. Kyle told the cult how they should shoot the teachers and the kids on their list, then burn the school down. Burning the school was a new idea to the group, one that was well received and made Kyle proud. Rudolph has a list of kids he likes and dislikes, those who should live and those who should die, that he constantly updates. He hands out revised editions every school day at lunch.

As Kyle waits for everyone to arrive he surfs the Internet. He orders the film *Dog Day Afternoon* from Amazon and puts it on his Mom's credit card. He's been thinking about some of the skater kids he knows, but the coolest ones are straight-edge, and smoking pot, or at least drinking—since Randolph won't smoke—seem like such an important part of the cult, so he can't ask them to join. One of the guys, Mick, shaves his head and is the only kid at their high school with a tattoo. Kyle thinks he has enough time to beat off before the meeting when the cell phone rings. He answers it, "Hello?"

"It's me again."

"Uh. Yeah."

"So. Do you still want to use me?"

Kyle thinks for a moment and says yes.

"Wait a minute. Someone's coming," the voice says and the phone goes dead. Just then Kyle's doorbell rings. Probably Randolph. He's always early. That's okay though, because now Kyle has a hard-on.

The meeting went exceptionally well. Half-way through their gathering Randolph had what doctors in movies call *a break-through*. Rachel had scored some ecstasy at the mall and she split half a hit with Randolph while Kyle took two hits, forgetting all about recruitment while he and Rachel spun into their synchronized swimming routine where they swim fully-clothed on the carpet, imitating the stoic bird movements they found so hysterical while watching the Olympics a few weeks ago. While they were doing leg-splits on their backs Daisy fumed in a corner, Randolph kept saying "hey, hey, hey." He had sunk so low into the beanbag only his knees and the *Sun and Steel* book shown, a wisp of blond hair the bookmark. Randolph sat up. His cheeks were flushed from the ecstasy, and he slammed the book shut to get their attention.

"*Hey*. Did you guys realize that this book was published when Mishima was *alive?* I was reading the biography on the back. It's in the *present tense*. Look, look." He holds up the book with an intense earnestness.

Kyle and Rachel stop their dry swimming and swing around on their buttocks to simultaneously face Randolph. Daisy pauses her Gameboy.

"*Look*," Randolph implores, handing them the book as he trips over his own feet, rushing to the pile of videos that bolster Kyle's TV.

"*Look*."

He then hands them the video box while taking the book back to expose the first page.

"*See?* This date of his suicide in the movie is only a couple of months after the book was published." Randolph's eyes are wide, his pupils dilated.

"He...he could have signed your book, Kyle. He could have signed it in blood!" At that the three of them collapse into an embrace shaking with tears, ecstasy percolating in their brains, their mission signed with the invisible, bloody kiss of fate. When they think Rachel isn't looking Kyle and Randolph give each other little furtive kisses.

Daisy puts her Gameboy in her backpack, announces that she has to get home before her ten o'clock curfew, and if Randolph still wants that ride he better say his good-byes now.

The three of them take her command seriously, hugging and weeping much as prisoners might at the end of visiting hour. And just like that they start laughing. Kyle walks the three of them outside to the driveway. The street lights pulse like giant fireflies moored against their will, their green halos angrily enlarge then recede with each passing car. He takes the book from Randolph but before he can say goodbye Daisy reaches across, pulls the door shut, steps on the gas and roars down the street. Rachel looks up at him from in her car. He thinks he should say 'I love you,' or at least 'Drive safe.'

Kyle smiles absently and says "I gotta go."

In his room he thinks about turning on some music or maybe the television. After his cult left he did two huge lines of Ritalin along with a few shots of Nyquil while playing some new Japanese video game, *Store Detective*, that Randolph bought on-line, one where you shoot shoplifters, losing points if you wing a salesgirl or a kill a shopper. Kyle's vision is so blurred he just shoots, hoping for the best. He is out of pot so he rips the filter off a Kool and smokes it fast. Sitting in his room, trying to decide between turning on some music or maybe the television, the cell phone rings.

"It's me."

"Uh," Kyle's throat is dry, sanded by the fiberglass peppermint of the Menthol cigarette. Pause. "Uh. Do you want to come over?"

"Darling, I'm already here."

Kyle laughs a short laugh and swallows, trying to get his voice to work again.

"Very funny. Fuck you."

"No, no. First we have to hold hands."

Kyle still recognizes the voice. It is *the* voice. But clear, loud, almost with an echo, as if it were coming from the next room.

"Uh. Where are you?"

"The next room."

Kyle looks around.

Pause.

"Where *are* you?"

"Leave your room and walk down the hall."

Kyle smirks. He knows this is a game. He'll play. *Big Deal.* He opens his door and looks out into the hall. Whenever he's this high the hallway always has this familiar tilt.

"So where are you?"

"In your parent's room."

"No shit?" Kyle giggles, "Like, in bed with them?" Kyle does an exaggerated, cartoonish tiptoe down the hall and puts an ear against the door.

He doesn't know what to do.

"Open the door." Now a flat whisper, as Kyle hesitates, the voice again says, "Open the door."

Kyle opens the door, throwing a rectangle of light across the bunched quilt covering his parents, torsos oddly exposed, heads beneath a mass of pillows wrested from their covers. An arm of indiscernible parentage anchors the whole thing down. Kyle looks around.

"I'm under the bed." Kyle turns off the phone. He looks at the form of his parents beneath the darkness and sheets. The digital glow of the alarm clock showers stationary red comets across the thrust of his mother's hair resting between sheet and pillow. With one hand lightly on the mattress he gets down on his knees and peers under the bed.

The light from the hall cuts a clear, empty swath beneath the stressed box springs. Nothing there but his father's shiny Colt .45,

fully loaded, always loaded, straining against its black vinyl holster.
Kyle reaches for the gun.

Pause.

LOWBEAR

Village boys woke at dawn to rush the sparse woods. The hills surrounding the village had long been stripped bare, denuded of all foliage but the toughest, inedible twist of raw roots. Mothers would strap their sons with nearly empty backpacks weighted with compacted rice balls and weathered water bags while fathers licked thumbs and rubbed the sleep out of their son's eyes. Kit struggled to corral knots of cold, sticky rice with his chopsticks as his father renewed the hearth with kindling and bark. Along with the other boys, he scoured the wastes for metal while his parents worked the rice fields. On his return trip he would search the ground for any available firewood. The village youth had to go farther and farther to find the valuable scraps of metal, the lifeblood of the village, making it harder to return by nightfall.

And with nightfall came the Lowbear.

Village boys raced the sinking sun to beat the fearful Lowbear. Behind barred doors, in shushed homes, they emptied their packs of any metal or wood they might have scavenged. In the morning fathers turned over the bounty to the Blacksmiths, whose works kept the village in tools while providing them with valuable trade items when they went calling on other communities.

The guild of Blacksmiths was at the center of the village, literally and figuratively. They were the keepers of the flame, kneading metal, heating it until it was a liquid orange drooling happy sparks, fashioning hardy tools, but they did not know how to make metal. Metal was found in the ground, far from the village, in the devastated crater of an ancient city. There were such craters close to the village, much smaller of course, perfect circles filled with water, ideal for terraced rice farming. Those that did not fill with water shimmered with clover in the short spring, and made for a natural catch-all for kindling in the fall and long winter. The village boys passed these in a steady, deliberate run. The crater they aimed for could not be missed as it was so large that the perimeter could not be traversed in a single day, nor could you see the other edge, only a terrible ellipse was perceptible, the dark crush of impact that left nothing but shards of dusty metal. Nothing grew here. The village elders had long ago decided that the unnaturally white sand of the crater was in actuality the ash from an uncountable number of skulls pulverized in the Red War. And so boys dutifully washed in the pools outside the village before returning to their homes, lest eviscerated spirits take up residence in their chimneys.

Kit's father had told him that in the past the entire village would come and collect the metal; they would rake the ashy sand and find any number of peculiar items to sell at market in the villages past the mountains. But as the winters lengthened it became harder and harder to harvest enough rice; it was more difficult, too, to find things of value in the waste, so the search became the responsibility of the village boys, youths energetic enough to make it home before dark. With darkness the villagers locked their doors and sat in silence as the beast prowled the streets.

The Blacksmiths did not lock their doors at night. Their stable of fire and smoke was without doors, at the center of town, the clanging of their hammers announced the morning. Night began with this hiss of dirty water steaming off their hot forges. They were the only men who did not return home to their families in the evening. They were their own family, a family of men and it was considered an honor in the village to contribute a boy to the guild. If a child seemed sturdy and large he might apprentice with them; as he grew, if he could handle fire and shape metal, if he took to their brotherhood of work song and secret oaths, he would be allowed to stay and grow the beard that symbolized their trade and camaraderie. Kit had often snuck looks toward their stone and brick den, aglow in hearth fire at day's end. He was drawn to their warm weariness as they shuffled off to the bathhouse, large, raw hands on muscled shoulders, soot on their cheeks blended into the darkness of their beards. Kit strained to observe as much of their interaction as he could, hoping to penetrate their secrets in the fleeting moments as he passed by on his way from the fields of scrap, where the boys did not laugh or talk but grimly competed, ever watchful that they beat the sinking sun home.

The Lowbear started entering the village that past winter. Kit's family, as every family in the village, gathered close to the hearth and ate in silence. In the past this was a time for storytelling and pipe smoking and games with the children as families took turns visiting one another. Now silence was solemnly observed so as not to attract the beast. His father had often and proudly told the entire family that *his* father's father had hunted the last of the bears from the hills, that they were small and smart and dangerous only when you crossed them with their young. Their pelts had fetched a fortune at market. But the Lowbear was different. Some elders fretted that it was an evil spirit, here to wreak vengeance on the hunters' descendants; others argued that the Lowbear was a monster coming to the village to reclaim stolen metal it deemed precious. Kit's family believed this. Strange things are born of the crater, though Kit thought the elders' insistent talk that the small beaked hillbirds darting in and out of their burrows in the crater walls, once flew was a fable. The only things that could fly were festival kites and the fist-sized summer locusts. Other boys agreed with him; they'd labored to catch one of the little beasts. Upon examining its scaly feet and fluffy fingerless arms, obviously perfect for digging, they dismissed the elders' stories as amusement at their expense.

The creature had first been spotted at dusk, lingering near the rice patties. Some of the younger men had wanted to organize a hunting party. The monster was described as walking upright, like a man, or a spirit. That this might be an altogether different beast gave them pause. Events of the following evening proved them right.

A family on the outskirts of the village was recently new with child; the baby's cries awoke the family and alerted them to an alarming presence filling their doorway. The father quick-wittedly stuck a broom into the fireplace and as it burst into flame waved it at the monster. And this was the only close look anyone had of the Lowbear, so named by the frightened farmer because its neckless head hung low, nearly even with its massive shoulders, a protruding lower jaw sprouted black teeth that caged an equally ebony human-like skull punctuated by intelligent eyes ablaze in sad curiosity. The beast turned and closed the door behind him with an all-too-human hand. And so the elders divided over whether the creature was supernatural or a monster, not that they could question the farmer any further. He moved his family to the village of Glassblowers the next morning.

It was argued that the Blacksmiths, being the biggest, strongest men, should hunt the creature, but this was quickly dismissed; one of their creeds is that though they made tools, their talents were for building, not destroying. Some whispered that this ancient rule resulted from their ancestors' participation in the the ancient conflict that, eons ago, left the world a patchwork of craters. They called the conflict the Red War because it drowned every city in blood while setting the sky afire. Blacksmith elders countered that the guild opposed the war and took their ways into the mountains to preserve them, returning to help rebuild the shattered villages. The continued glow of their forge kept the Lowbear from penetrating the heart of the village.

In the morning Kit headed toward the crater. The air was moist with dew; he could see his breath. Fall was near. At either side other boys ran, each set on reaching the giant bowl as quickly as possible. They tended to fan out the closer they got to the crater. Adults could not run as fast or as far to reach the crater and return by dusk, so the boys were instructed to avoid each other and spread out, to insure that both a lot of ground was covered and to keep the unsupervised youths from fighting over scrap. Every time Kit reached the rim he paused to take in the view. It never failed to impress.

The world dropped away in a clean, crisp circular line, like a giant spoon had scooped out miles and miles of earth. The elders claimed that this too came from the sky, that the sky was once dominated by men who traveled by air. A beaked hillbird twisted its tiny head out of its hovel and peered up at him, then just as quickly retracted itself. *Flight*. The Red War obviously took many things from the earth, but the fancies of flight that obsessed the elders gave Kit reason to shake his head before he started his descent. Even his father admitted that he didn't believe every tale the village elders wove, but he'd also told his son that when he was his age, his father had taken him on a long journey to trade at a large city far from their village, and that the city's walls were adorned with gigantic metal spears, battered totems of past violence. These ancient weapons glowed faintly at night and illuminated the tumorous, misshapen beggars perched below.

When Kit reached the basin he walked with his eyes on the ground. Nothing grew here, and though the region closest to the rim had been picked clean by foraging boys, every rain might produce a new find. Though they could get glass from the village of Glassblowers, it was an expensive trade, so they were alert for glass as well; an unbroken bottle was as valuable as a chunk of iron. He scoured the ground for hours. Resting against a massive rise of rock, Kit drank greedily from his water bag and ate most of his rice balls, reminiscing about the roast locus dipped in honey he'd had last summer, during Long Day festival. Another boy, Tung, approached. Tung was big for his age and lorded it over the other boys. Kit was glad he hadn't found anything yet because Tung would badger smaller boys into trading their finds for paltry ones. Kit greeted the other boy with a grunt as he moved to the same rock to sun himself.

.

The sun was now high and the rock had heated up. After they exchanged gossip, Tung removed his shirt and placed his hands behind his head and drifted off to sleep. Kit tried not to stare. Tung had grown since last winter and there were two black paintbrushes of hair lapping his underarms. Tung opened his eyes and caught Kit studying him. He raised an eyebrow and grinned as Kit blushed and lowered his head, angry that the older boy had been feigning sleep, that he would mistake his curiosity for admiration, or something else.

"I've got hair in other places as well."

Tung slid down the rock and was now looking up at Kit. Kit scanned the barren horizon. Not another boy was in sight.

"And look at this." Tung slapped his round stomach and lowered his pants. He started to piss against the rock, still grinning at Kit.

"I've got hair here too, now, and my *bun chow* has grown. I bet I'll have a beard next year, too, so I can join the Blacksmiths."

Kit doubted the Blacksmiths would take such a sour kid as Tung or that he'd even have the first sprout of a beard anytime soon, but he couldn't stop staring at the dark nest of his crotch. Tung finished urinating but had not bothered to fasten his pants. He stood with his legs wide apart, dirty hands on his hips, admiring his growing *bun chow*. Kit was hypnotized. He had only seen his father's *bun chow* up close at the bathhouse, the sight of which made him yearn to visit the Blacksmith's gigantic, private tub. Tung wagged his hips.

"Yes, I'm getting bigger." He lowered his voice, "You see, whenever my mother isn't looking, I eat from my sister's bowl. She's too afraid of me to say anything, and I want to get big enough to be a Blacksmith."

Kit made a noncommittal noise and turned before Tung could say another word. He scampered back up the rock and down the other side. Whatever it took to become a Blacksmith, stealing from family was despicable. Bitterness replaced the intrigue and excitement that had coursed through his body just moments ago. It was past noon and he'd yet to find anything of value. He redoubled his efforts so not to return empty-handed.

By the time he'd finally found something of value, a priceless coin, the sun was low. He felt it getting colder.

Kit raced home, clutching the coin. Coins were not melted down, but traded to rich men in the larger villages, often times for something as valuable as a goat. Some elders wore coins on chains around their necks to remind them of their younger days, when coins were common. As he ran, he thought about presenting the coin to the Blacksmiths himself and inquiring if it was valuable; of course he knew it was, but it would be a good excuse to stop at their forge and look inside. *It had been over a year since he had tasted goat milk; his mother would cry tears of joy over their fortune.*

The sky bruised a darker shade of purple and the first of many stars to come flickered into view. Kit quickly abandoned any thought other than concentrating on the quickest route home; with dusk the Lowbear emerged. He shivered and became more acutely aware of the dropping temperature. As he crested a small hill, the village came into view. Kit had relaxed his stride when he noticed a dark shape rising between him and his destination. Fear filled him as he exhaled and sought to both further slow his sprint and choose a different direction without making his presence known. But the shape was closer than he initially thought.

The Lowbear approached. Huge arms swept up to engulf him— he opened his mouth to scream.

"Quiet!" His father shushed him and embraced him in a warming hug. He pulled his son under the blanket he had over his shoulders; that was what had deformed his shape in the growing darkness.

"Your mother was worried and sent me to look for you. Quickly, let's get back."

They turned toward the village. His father was so happy to see the boy he forgot to ask how the day's hunt had gone. Excited and relieved by his father's appearance, Kit forgot all about the coin. Only when his mother made him stand in a large pot so she could scrub him clean, did he unclench his fist and let it drop into the bowl with a splash. His astonished parents whooped for joy, then quickly lowered their voices and looked toward the barred door.

In the morning his father rewarded him with a surprise trip to the Bathhouse. He would then spend the day in the fields, to learn about planting and harvesting. A good day indeed. Kit's father steered the boy through the streets, stopping to talk to vendors, waving to friends on their way to the rice fields. Everyone greeted them boisterously, as a weekday trip to the Baths was a luxury.

The massive, wooden bathhouse, next to the forge, was the largest, oldest structure in the village. Built over a spring, large tubs were heated by hot rocks. Masseuses kneaded groans from their clients. Village elders played board games while ladling water over hot rocks. The weekends were for families but during weekdays the bathhouse was a place of men. All business, personal or concerning the town, took place within the tubs and steam rooms. They left their sandals at the door and bowed to the attendant. His father nodded to the men he was friendly with and loosened his robe while gathering his son's sash as well. As Kit's robe opened his father pulled it off him and folded it over his own. He then placed the palm of his hand on the small of his son's back.

"I need to speak to the elder-mayor about your wonderful find. Relax here until I come for you."

He gave him a gentle shove and with that Kit found himself alone and naked in the private bath of the Blacksmiths. Embarrassed and confused, he turned to follow his father, but instantly knew the trouble he'd be in if he disobeyed such a carefully worded command. There was nothing to do but step forward and climb up to the wide tub and ease himself into the water.

Several Blacksmiths lounged about, stroking their beards or dozing in the hot water. Islands of large toes and strong tanned bellies broke the water. Kit lowered himself in and gripped the smooth wooden seat, holding as much of his body underwater as possible. Only his eyes and nose broke the surface.

"Look at this. I think we're all stewing in turtle soup," the nearest Blacksmith announced. The others chuckled.

The burly Blacksmith turned to rest his massive arms on the ledge of the tub. "Do me a favor, turtle, scrub my back."

A meek Kit obeyed and paddled over to the sweating behemoth. The Blacksmith threw a rag over his shoulder and the boy caught it and began scrubbing the immense, dripping landscape before him. He nearly swooned from steam and nervousness but was brought back to the task at hand when the Blacksmith growled. "Harder."

This room seemed even older than the others, more cave-like, and the ceiling was lower. Kit thought he could make out the remnants of a faded mural: greens and reds, the faint figures of strong men. He sensed a struggle; but nothing was left of the ancient paints but the faintest of impressions.

"Turtle, why do we Blacksmiths twist metal, why do we make things?"

Kit was surprised by the question and didn't know how to answer. He wondered if his father had put him in here as a test, one that he was about to fail.

"You don't know? Well neither do I." The giant Blacksmith rolled over, blunt toes poked out of the water as his wake washed over Kit. "I think we just like to make things, make things together." He smiled. Kit nodded.

"You should come to the forge one evening. I'll show you how to work an iron." The boy beamed in eager gratitude as his father appeared in the doorway, motioning for him to join him in the steam room.

That night Kit had trouble falling asleep, and not for the usual fear that the Lowbear prowled nearby. Excitement burned in his mind. He got up, wrapped a blanket around himself and squatted by the low flame of the hearth. Carefully, he took the coin from its hiding place beneath the salt bin and examined it. Worn smooth by the centuries, Kit could tell that it was special, different from most. Usually the coins they find in the crater had faded characters and numbers, but on this one he discerned the profile of a man on one side. He thought of the faded mural in the bathhouse. The reverse side held a strange creature, beaked like a hillbird, but its arms were alive, like fire; it looked as if it were about to rise. Kit went back to bed; as sleep fretfully descended, his mind churned with questions.

By the next morning, word of Kit's discovery had spread among the village boys. As he trudged through town, each boy raced up behind him and slapped him on the back for good luck. He said nothing until one boy hit him so hard he nearly lost his footing. He looked up in time to see Tung grinning maliciously back at him. Kit gave him a weak wave and paused to note his direction and to make sure he headed toward an entirely different part of the crater.

Kit reached the rim early, likely ahead of the other boys; a new determination fueled his muscles and his mind. Images from the previous night's dreams kept rising to the surface: he was working along side the Blacksmiths. They guided him with their huge, caring hands to the fiery forge. A metallic hillbird screeched and strained against the Blacksmiths that held it down, sparks dripping from its molten tongue. He shook his head and slid down the embankment. He could not let dreams or his recent success distract him. Better to cover more ground than usual and to try and gather extra firewood on the way back home as the nights were getting colder.

He kept his eyes on the ground. Scratching loose dirt with a stick, he uncovered a small bottle. Though cracked it was still valuable. When he was younger he would have used this as an excuse to rush home early for an extra bowl of congee. But today he felt the need to keep digging, and only after some time did he look up and realize he was near the large rock he had shared with Tung yesterday.

And Tung was walking toward him. Kit groaned. He knew the other boy would think that this rendezvous was anything but accidental. He even thought about giving him a friendly wave and jogging off in the other direction, but something about Tung's gait stilled this thought. The other boy slumped and seemed listless. As he neared, Kit could make out confusion and possibly even fear on the boy's ashen face. He called out.

"Tung, what's a matter?"

The boy looked up as if he'd only just noticed Kit and shrugged. He looked over his shoulder, toward the foreboding center of the crater; in the summer shimmering waves of heat bent and distorted the sand and rock, radiating menace. Since the boys were under strict commands to return home by nightfall there was never time to explore this mysterious expanse.

Tung stuttered softly. "I-I… *really* wanted to find a coin after I saw you this morning. So I ran like I never ran before. I didn't bother to look down until I was out in the middle, out *there*."

He narrowed his eyes and studied the horizon in disbelief. Kit did the same but saw nothing. Tung rubbed his sweaty neck.

"I found something. I found a hole."

Kit knew what he was going to say next.

"I think it's where the Lowbear lives."

That night Kit ate in silence, speaking up only to ask for seconds, though he wasn't hungry. His mother worked the loom while his father smoked by the hearth. As he settled in among his blankets on the floor, he asked both his parents for the third time to wake him early. His father agreed, mussed his hair, and told him to get some sleep. Kit closed his eyes, thinking sleep unlikely. A pre-winter wind howled down the streets. He and Tung had agreed to meet before sunrise and to race to the rim. They would try to locate the hole again, marking the path with stones so they could return again with the men of the village. Then they would be responsible for the capture or death of the monster, earning them a spot among the Blacksmiths! Tung demanded the bottle Kit had found as the price for sharing in the secret. Kit didn't mind, but as the wind wrapped around their small home and scratched at the chimney, all he could think about was the Lowbear outside, enraged over the boy's coming trespass; it's black, human fingers reaching for the door.

His mother shook him awake while his father still slept. Kit had never been up this early, and blinked at the amount of silent preparation his mother put into breakfast. At the door he bowed deeply in appreciation. She waved away such formality but smiled broadly, pushing her hair up and back under her frayed kerchief as Kit unbarred the door and slipped outside.

Tung was waiting for him.

They jogged toward the rim. Sunrise flared, baking the hills hues of dark purple. Once in the basin Tung marched ahead, stopping every so often to dig out a large stone, placing it in line with others to mark their path. Far beyond the large rock where they had first plotted this adventure, farther than Kit had ever thought to travel, Tung paused and pointed at the ground. Kit stared and after awhile could discern a pattern. The weave of rock beneath the sand was one of straight lines and sharp angles. He looked at Tung, who only nodded. They were standing in the midst of numerous foundations. The dusty outline of city spread beneath their feet.

"I think those big storms last summer washed enough dirt away. Don't tell anyone, but I've been coming out here for a few weeks now. I've found bits of metal but not much else, not until the other day."

He motioned for Kit to follow. Kit hesitated. Yesterday Tung had said he'd only just gone this far into the waste and now he was saying he had been here before. But curiosity urged him along. After walking through what Kit thought must be a maze of Tung's imagining, the pattern of city streets became discernable; the ground was unnaturally smooth and even. And then Tung turned an invisible corner and pointed toward a hole in the ground.

The gaping blackness struck Kit as artificial, angular, wrong, a doorway into darkness; he was compelled to drop his bag and flee. Tung looked scared. Kit didn't care if the older boy thought he was a coward. He backed away, then searched the horizon: the rim was so far off he could easily perceive the crater's monstrous circumference.

He turned back around and Tung was gone.

Kit's heartbeat doubled and a troubling dryness hollowed his mouth and throat. He desperately wanted his father to appear, along with the men of the village, to explain where Tung was, why this horrible black pit existed and then lead him home.

Tung popped his head out of the darkness and frantically waved Kit over. Tung crouched on the first two steps of a stairwell and put his finger to his lips for silence. Kit wanted to grab him and together flee the mouth of the Lowbear lair; their discovery was enough, they need go no further. But Tung motioned with his other hand, pointing down the stairwell, toward a faint light. Boyish interest dampened his fear as Kit took a tentative step down, then another. Tung clutched his arm and they descended.

The stairwell was short, ending in a wide pool of sand that thinned out onto a hard floor—obviously the push of rain and weather had shifted earth, once again exposing this black cavity. Kit wondered if this resulted in the release of the Lowbear. The boys paused to let their eyes adjust to the dim light. They were in a small room with metal bars that hung floor to ceiling on one side. This was enough metal to enrich their village for years. They shared a look of greed. Beyond the metal bars, a soft glow beckoned; faint voices could be heard. Kit wanted to ask Tung if he thought the Lowbear could talk, but swallowed the question and stepped forward. The walls were not rock, but seemed to be made of a substance similar to the ancient plates possessed by only the oldest families in the village. The minute squares swirled in shapes and patterns. The boys moved quietly toward the row of metal bars. The center was unobstructed, so they stepped through into the coolness of a tunnel.

Torchlight illuminated a dancing circle of Blacksmiths. Naked save leather loin clothes straining beneath hard bellies, the sweat beading off their beards caught the flicker of light like jewels. They chanted together in a joyous rapture, in a private language the boys found both alien and inviting.

The curvature of the walls revealed mosaics that mirrored the ceiling of the bathhouse in color and complexity, but were more vivid, even in the relative darkness, than those of the baths; most likely, they had been preserved in the cool manmade cavern for eons. Preserved, but not untouched. Kit noticed additions to the artwork, stories painted on stories. Pictograms of men huddling in the hills as the sky burned. Drawings showed burly Blacksmiths digging a well, with the village represented by just a few huts, and the forge under construction. Older depictions, fiery etchings of wild creatures, flying spirits, drew the boys closer. They stepped down into the tunnel, holding hands for comfort and support. The ground was divided by continuous bolts of metal; more treasure. Kit wondered if that the tunnel stretched back to the village, if it opened beneath the Blacksmiths' forge.

It would be days before he would consider what might lie in the other direction.

The air was hot with the incense of animal breath. Sweat accumulated between their palms. An unkind roar shook the tunnel from behind as they approached the male frenzy before them. The men parted to let them join, swallowing the boys in mystery and initiation as torches flared. Fire licked ancient paint off the walls, burning the rock canvas clean in preparation for new, bold stories.

SUNDOWNERS

The repossession of Kathleen's car had been like a punch in the kidneys. They repo men had come when she was at church—not to pray but for the court-appointed substance abuse group. The rest of the addicts were mostly women. Kathleen didn't care for other women. They talked too much about their children for her liking. Kathleen preferred the company of men, though the line leading from friendship to bad sex had shortened to the point where she rarely desired those encounters either. Mary Ann was different, bold, as nurses always are, drinking her coffee in gulps and describing her hatred of the other women in their court-required substance abuse group so vividly Kathleen *had* to like her. Kathleen could tell she was a nurse. Her legs were thick and her sneakers as worn as an Olympic athletes'. Together, they would smoke during coffee breaks and even after group, sometimes letting the night linger into a late piece of pie at the diner across from the church where group met. Mary Ann had pretty much the same weakness, though Mary's had a wild bent; she'd liked heroin and had a husband whose chemical sweet tooth hankered for morphine as well. Morphine which Mary Ann stole, watering down the cancer ward's supply with saline solution, and sometimes tap water. Her husband was in jail now, and despite her rap sheet, the courts decided she'd do a better job at raising the kids. Having turned state's witness, she was on probation and a mouthful of methadone. When she had told her this one night Kathleen responded, "Well, if I had three kids I'd be on heroin too." Painful confession had eased into a natural friendship. She told Mary Ann her deepening money troubles.

Mary Ann nodded and listened. Kathleen had noticed that Mary Ann drove a BMW with tinted limousine windows, and she assumed some of the drug money must have been cached away. But Mary Ann admitted she had found a cushy job as a private nurse, one that paid too well.

After Kathleen's car was repo'd, Mary Ann looked at Kathleen for a full minute, with such a deep look of measurement, that Kathleen supposed she was a dyke after all.

"I'm sorry. I might be able to get you an interview with people with more money than God. Just as scary." Mary Ann took Kathleen's hand in hers. "I'm not allowed to talk about work. I signed some forms."

Kathleen thanked her and, next group, changed tack. Instead of coffee, they went for drinks. Mary Ann drove. They went to a nice little blues bar Kathleen knew in Burlington. There were enough college students there that the men there wouldn't bother them, which was fine. Kathleen wanted to get Mary Ann drunk, drunk and talking. By the second pitcher, she found out Mary Ann was making more money than half the doctors Kathleen had known at the hospital. Shots of whiskey revealed that Mary Ann wasn't a private nurse, but on staff at an exclusive retirement home, one with an impressive research facility as well. Mary Ann sobered up after realizing she had talked perhaps a bit too much and looked Kathleen directly in the eye.

"You need to understand, these are the fucking oldest, richest people in the world. And they didn't get this far or this rich by being sweet."

Kathleen began swearing her confidence to Mary Ann, but Mary Ann just waved her away.

"Uh-uh, darling. You'll sink or swim on your own. I've just done the introduction. If you're hired you're hired on your own and I'll get a huge bonus if you stay on. I guess I can tell you I hated the woman who recommended me, hated her guts once I realized what she'd gotten me into. I told her, I said to her, do you realize what you've gotten me into? And she said, Yeah, the most interesting place on earth. You know, after a few months I decided she was right. Now let's dance while I can still find my feet."

Kathleen drove toward the clinic for her third interview. They knew everything about her, and still asked her back, called her in the middle of the night with more questions. *Shit, they even know about the stuff I was sure no one caught me doing,* she thought while rolling the window down to extinguish her cigarette on the underside of her side-view mirror, letting the butt drop. They knew about the prescription drugs. They knew about the conviction. Worse, they knew how many times she'd beat the charges. During the second interview they questioned her at length about the credit card fraud. The questions so astute that she worried she had been drawn into a sting operation and had asked repeatedly if her interviewers where cops. They were not, they assured her, with smiles she in no way found comforting. The questions asked over the phone were medical, painfully meticulous, true tests. Thankfully, she had a minor in hematology, with specific training over the years in transfusion and dialysis, to fend off the tougher questions. The phone interviews lasted hours. Not that she cared. Kathleen needed this job. She had taken and passed two lie detector tests at two different agencies, had the appropriate transcripts forwarded, bought new hose. She needed this job.

As she turned down the gravel drive, Kathleen admitted to herself that she had been intrigued, a new emotion for her after years of suspicion, weariness, and withdrawal. She gave brief, exact answers to the medical questions over the phone. During the in-person interviews she had told them everything, after all they seemed to know everything, but here her pride showed through. She had been shrewd in her theft. She had stolen the drugs that made her feel silver inside. She had stolen countless identities and credit cards to pay every conceivable bill, from lawyer bills to over fifty pairs of shoes. When those were impounded as evidence, she realized she did not have any shoes to wear for her next court date so she bought two pairs of Prada on a fresh credit card in the name of a patient who had regretfully passed away under her care that past Christmas. Her interviewers laughed at that one. And they paid her for these interviews; enough to get her car back and catch up on rent, get the dawning gray professionally colored out of her hair.

The interviewers, a consortium of doctors and nurses, had seemed nonplussed by anything criminal. She had the weird feeling they were pleased by her past. Maybe they wanted something on her, turning her into an indentured servant. They were clear from the start: the clinic demanded privacy. Kathleen would not be required to do anything illegal. She would, however, have to sign nondisclosure forms so stringent and completely legal she could be fired and sued for using the word "clinic" during a game of Scrabble.

The clinic came into view. It occupied a vast Venetian Palace that had been brought over from Italy and rebuilt, brick by brick, by a wealthy family some two hundred years back, not an uncommon occurrence for this area of Long Island. The clinic had taken over the grounds more than fifty years ago. This part of Long Island was know as a playground of the rich but reclusive. The guards at both check points seemed young and care-free, dispensing with those ridiculous quasi-military uniforms most security guards are required to wear. Except for the perfect physiques and the semiautomatic weapons they leisurely hefted about, they almost looked like fraternity kids doing community service, wearing khakis and open collared Izods. They knew her by her first name the first time she approached the gate. *I'm going to like it here*, she thought, parking the car casually in front of the main entrance. *As long as they don't have me pulling kidneys out of runaways and plugging them into rich old matrons, I'll do anything for the cash they're going to throw at me.*

She pushed her hair behind her ears and looked at her reflection in the rearview mirror. The few, premature gray hairs missed by the salon had a healthy, silver hue. She decided she liked this bit of color creeping into her part, giving her personality a more serious tone. She checked her teeth for flecks of lipstick, took a deep breath and allowed herself a moment, a moment only, of serious apprehension before her final interview.

Touring the ward, the head nurse explained, quite firmly, that they were not called patients, but rather *guests*. She had spent most of the morning in a series of lectures with two physicians who had such an uncanny resemblance to one another it made their message all the more surreal. They had different last names, but the same corpulence, same wild, black mustaches and similar bad haircuts. One was taller. The one who went by Dr. Mike seemed to be the more diffident of the two, and never used her name. The other, Dr. Bob, used her name and used it often. Most likely a trick he'd picked up at a seminar for doctors who wished to pass as human. Both traits annoyed her, though the information she was expected to absorb was so overwhelming as to dwarf any opinion forming in the back of her mind. The forefront of her mind was mostly occupied by one long scream: *Get-the-hell-out-of-here.* Yet their science was as baffling as it was captivating, and the weird duality of their matching tone and cadence was a bit hypnotic as well. Nothing they said could possibly be real, though every effort had been made to link it to the realm of probability. Now the tour: room after room of dialysis machines. Though these machines were like nothing she'd seen before. Sleek, half the size of the equipment she'd been exposed to, prototypes designed and built on the premises, each uniquely fitted to encapsulate their prospective guest. The guests looked ancient. Their protruding, pale, often bald heads were composed. A few napped open-mouthed, a gnarled fang exposed.

The serenity on each face strongly suggested that this dialysis *felt* good. *No,* she reminded herself. *Not good. Nourishing.* She tentatively leaned in to examine an antique face. She'd been reassured constantly, from the onset of the tour, that they were harmless in this state, harmless indeed, throughout the term of their care. That aspect of their existence, what was once so violently harmful, had faded. The guests were at the end of their incredibly long lives. *Correction, not life. Existence.* It was going to be her job to provide comfort for the harbingers of permanent twilight. Still feeling as if there were an element of charade here, she surveyed the room. The huge Baroque ceilings were in cavernous contrast to the row of identical, rather small capsules. She tentatively stroked the leathery, cool brow of the nearest reclining vampire as the head nurse looked on with an approving nod.

Her first six months were all day shift. This was a prerequisite for the nursing staff, and on her first night shift Kathleen could see why. Day shift was a careful monitoring of the dialysis machines; a break was assisting the research staff. Their work with plasma brought in grants which gave the clinic an existence in the real world, allowing for the medical equipment needed to make the guests comfortable. From the other nurses she found out that, yes, the guests had families, families, of course, of similar disposition, but thankfully the clinic had no visiting hours. Kathleen learned this was at the request of the families, not the clinic.

"Imagine how much more frightening death must be to an immortal?" Mary Ann said over dinner. The clinic had pulled some strings to get them both out of group. Mary Ann worked the night shift since Kathleen had started, so they rarely met at work. Their friendship deepened. Each now felt as if they had a confidant in the conspiracy of their lives. Kathleen loved moving from her crummy little apartment in Vermont to a condo on Long Island. She couldn't wait for summer; the beach was only a ten-minute drive away. The women she worked with were the kind of women she liked. Older women who mostly kept to themselves, the kind who didn't need to marry or had buried a husband and didn't feel like wearing out another. Nobody judged anybody. She liked that most of all. And nobody, not even Mary Ann, had bothered to warn her about the night shift.

During the night shift, the guests came alive. Each, of course, had, in their limited capacity, a different definition of living. Those guests confined to the West Wing were gently ushered out of their coffins (that's what *everyone* called the dialysis machines; the clinic had the same gallows humor all hospitals shared) and into a stately ballroom. Several of the guests still had a measure of their faculties. They played chess, or listened to chamber music played by a chamber quartet. Quite a few of the night nurses were fluent in European languages (two were former nuns and knew Latin and were quite stuffy about it) and would cut the cards, see to their individual needs. Few guests spoke English; fewer spoke much to the staff, preferring to sit in their little cliques in sumptuous robes, sipping clear plasma from crystal glasses rather inelegantly through plastic straws.

Apparently, existence over a thousand year period bred a patience and expertise for music unknown to the average human. The quartet was incredibly versatile, and though Kathleen knew nothing about classical music, she was occasionally moved. One night one of the musicians, a young woman who played the violin, brought in a glass harmonica—a long crystalline tube. Wetting her fingers in a bowl, she lightly stroked the ethereal harmonica. This elicited an otherworldly sound that reverberated throughout the clinic. One of the European nurses, seeing how enraptured Kathleen was, told her later the piece was written for the glass harmonica by Beethoven, commissioned by the count seated closest to the stage (more gallows humor: the nurses call male guests "count" and female guests "countess").

The East Wing was more dynamic. The thirst for blood elongated the lives of vampires but did not make them permanent. Entropy reigned, in the end. Though it took thousands of years, vampires did decline. It was like Alzheimer's; they eventually suffered a slow decay, first in faculty, then physically. They faced their final sunset usually while in their electric coffins, expiring in an exhalation of dust, that, though Kathleen had yet to witness, other nurses had told her sounded like a lifetime's worth of relief. In the East Wing as well, the dead were not dead yet. Farther along in their decline, these now completely-muted-guests were more active physically, slowly going through transformations that appeared incredibly uncomfortable to Kathleen. Dr. Bob, who apparently never slept and was always on hand, assured her that the guests were not hurting themselves. Indeed, for them it was fun, play. After getting used to the sights in the East Wing, Kathleen realized that here, like the ER on a Saturday night, she was more gentle bouncer than nurse. Near dawn, she would spend an hour or more coaxing countesses down from the ceiling. They would stubbornly cling to the ceiling, grey skin hanging off their bones like the weathered fabric of a ruined kite. In the East Wing it was harder to tell the counts from the countesses, because both were so similar in their thinness, hunched postures, bald skulls and shiny skin. Only a few, to Kathleen's disappointment, had pointy ears. Every night several of the counts tried to will themselves into wolf-form. The exertion was so trying that upon attaining wolf shape they collapsed into the deepest slumber, leg occasionally twitching, no doubt, with dreams of village maidens drained beneath their once long teeth. One poor count could only manage the hindquarters of a wolf, and with a raspy howl pulled himself across the floor in an odd, half-crouch, wagging a short, pathetic tail. The countesses all preferred to climb the walls and ceilings. Some of them sprouted a bit of webbing at their armpits, irritated by the robes that they shrugged off with the glee of a child escaping a towel after a bath. "Don't vampires fly?" Kathleen initially asked Dr. Bob.

"Oh, thankfully that's the first thing to go," he replied.

This amount of supervision required more vigilance, though none of the staff in the East or West Wing were at any risk. The guests had mostly lost their fangs by the time they took up residence. Their constant daytime feeding while in their coffins insured they were utterly satiated by sunset. Regardless, each nurse was outfitted with several thin leather turtlenecks to wear beneath their uniforms. The only staff members who didn't seem at ease were the small army of Filipino orderlies deployed every morning. After the guests were put down into their humming coffins, their long, twisting nails were filed down. By nightfall the countesses had re-grown their nails just enough to climb the marble walls, enough to cling to existing nicks rather than scrape out new ones. The orderlies wore crosses tucked into their uniforms and chatted nervously among themselves until their task was completed. Kathleen thought they should have all first taken a turn in a more typical retirement home. *Bedpans are a thousand times worse.*

On the second story, above the East Wing's nocturnal playground, within the research lab, more *interesting* guests were interred. An Indonesian vampire was here on an extended visit, inquiring about potential treatment for a maddening case of insomnia, which, for vampires, was undead hell. He occasionally joined a reluctant Dr. Bob in the West Wing for a midnight game of chess, but preferred to remain alone or in consultation with physicians. When Kathleen first saw him, she was surprised he was dressed in traditional Muslim garb. She assumed vampires were not religious. Dr. Bob had corrected this. "No, just not Christian, my dear."

Well, excuse me, Kathleen thought. With her hematology background, Kathleen was often in the research lab with a quick question or to replenish supplies for the coffins below. This was how she occasionally had access to the Cleopatra.

The Cleopatra, aside from the sleepless Indonesian, was the only guest afforded private quarters. The room had obviously been the Master Bedroom before the mansion had been converted into a clinic. The room was decorated in a muted Egyptian style, with gold wallpaper and a stunning fireplace in the shape of a miniature Sphinx, mouth wide, ready to breathe raging fire. The Cleopatra rested on a long, marble Beaux Arts dining room table without chairs in the center of the room. Ensconced in an unadorned glass vase, the Cleopatra swirled, an encapsulated red ocean of mystery. The large, simple vase was home to the clinic's oldest guest. Nothing was known about it, or her. The Cleopatra had earned her name not by her surroundings, which are more fitting than defining. Eternity had reduced this ancient vampire to nearly a mist. All that remained visible were a floating pair of ageless, clear eyes of infinite beauty.

The Cleopatra would not accept plasma, turning her small sea a defiant, angry purple if the pollutant were introduced. Pure, fresh blood was poured in the way a gardener might water a rare flower, the last of its kind. Both Dr. Mike and Dr. Bob did this together everyday at noon. No other staff was allowed to feed the Cleopatra.

Kathleen happened by the Cleopatra's room one evening and decided to take a peek. As she walked into the room she felt the eyes upon her. Kathleen was not afraid; she did not feel as if she were trespassing. She felt *welcome*. After all, Kathleen was a new sight. *Certainly, she's as sick of Dr. Mike and Dr. Bob as I am.* The eyes seemingly bobbed in agreement. Kathleen smiled and stepped closer to examine the vase. It was of a simple, thick and clear glass with a large crystal stopper ending in a menacing point.

As she walked around the vase, the eyes casually followed her. Kathleen breathed deeply. She had that *silvery* feeling in her blood that only the right pills and whisky ever summoned. Kathleen wanted to go barefoot, to lie before the fireplace and stick her head in the Sphinx's mouth, all for the amusement of the Cleopatra. Kathleen composed herself. Heading toward the door, she took one last look. But the eyes were gone, receded into the crimson storm, a jar of Jupiter's permanent weather.

Kathleen often visited the Cleopatra. She thought of asking the Doctors if she could feed her, but knew the question would raise suspicion. She imagined they tossed in the blood the way you poured milk out for a stray cat, not caring if any were spilt, just another chore. Sometimes she darkly imagined that they dripped the blood in slowly, lovingly, as a soothing cocktail for the Cleopatra.

Maybe they opened their own veins for her. She decided to check their wrists.

To Kathleen's surprise, she realized she had been with the clinic for one year. She got an excellent review from Dr. Bob and a good raise. Mary Ann took her to dinner. They talked about taking a vacation together, with all the wild abandon of plans made with no intention of ever being carried out. More surprising was how the clinic had quickly become routine. Instinctively, she knew from her ER experience, that such a feeling precipitates disaster. Still, the lull of routine overpowered premonition. That and they had been warned. After all, the winter solstice was the longest night of the year. The guests would be awake for their longest duration. Kathleen favored keeping them locked in their coffins, but realized this was probably unnecessarily cruel. Everyone knew their shift would be extended by an hour, nothing they weren't used to from their old jobs. Everyone took a roll-up-your-sleeves attitude. In the end, the guests were not the problem. An insomniac was.

The Indonesian vampire was still seeking treatment. He had left and come back, more irritable then ever. His English, after two centuries, was still pretty rusty. He thought all of the nurses were maids and would snap his long, yellow fingers at them whenever the craving for plasma hit him. He stopped playing chess with Dr. Bob, which irritated Kathleen; it was easier visiting the Cleopatra when she could be sure where the Doctors were. The visiting vampire however, had taken up an obnoxious habit of playing tennis on the ceiling with a countess.

He had discovered one of the countesses, though out of her mind, still retained a good backhand. They would play, suspended by their sharp, bare toes, from the East Wing ceiling every night for hours. Kathleen thought the countess looked rather ignoble, with her withered, upside down breasts flapping about, but she won as often as she lost, so none of the nurses voiced any serious complaint.

On the evening of the solstice, the Indonesian vampire had perhaps played tennis too long. Tired, in a desperate attempt to put the countess off her game, he hit the ball too far. It crashed though one of the stained glass windows. The noise it produced awoke several of the counts who had been resting far past their usual sleep. Their change always brought about an exertion that left them down until dawn. Tonight they awoke with the fresh scents of forest wafting though the broken glass. The night called and several counts transformed; in wolf shape, with a quick trot and an invigorated leap, some were actually able to escape before the nurses closed the electric storm windows. Chaos reigned. The silent alarm was sounded. Those guards not charged with securing the grounds rushed in to assess the problem. The excitement this elicited from the countesses made several of them attempt flight. They crashed to the ground and whimpered like old babies. Scrambling around on their knees, mingling with the wolfish were counts too deaf to have been wakened by the racket. Nurses quickly readied the coffins. Kathleen quietly mounted the stairs to the research lab.

First, she went to the bathroom to adjust her hair and make sure she didn't have lipstick flecked on her teeth. While looking in the mirror she unbuttoned the top button of her uniform. She listened by the door as the Indonesian vampire flew past and locked himself in his suite.

Kathleen walked into the Cleopatra's room.

Every time they were together, the silvery feeling returned and stayed, resonating giddily throughout her blood, lasting until the next day, the next visit. Moreover, the silvery feeling began to have a slight sound, a calling in the back of her mind. When she heard it, she was reminded of the glass harmonica, how it produced a seamless sound filling the room without any real discernable source. This was different. Here the source was as obvious and central as the sun.

She circled the vase slowly, teasingly tracing the lip of the stopper with one finger. The eyes within did not follow, they remained lazily fixed on the future. Kathleen removed the stopper. Music overwhelmed her. She raised the vase above her head in a baptismal toast to the thirsty night.

LOTUS BREAD

We hunt for shells, pretty ones. Some are broken but we don't care. Farther up the beach, the boy starts a small fire with driftwood and bits of a broken up picnic table. Not that it's cold, the boy just likes to stir the flames. Dorothea and I have filled our pail with shells so I guess we both know we should go home. I am hungry. She likes to stand ankle-deep in the water, staring out at the ocean. Her face and shoulders are bronze from our trips to the beach. At night I love the taste of salt from the ocean and her sweat that has crystallized on her brow. Her hair is longer, more blonde now, like the sprig of hair that has only recently sprung from my chin. She stares out at the sea with the same unhooked intensity with which the boy looks at fire.

If I remember, tonight I'll ask him his name.

We walk across the bridge as the sun sets. There are a few other people heading back from shore. Some families have fished all day and proudly show each other their catch. I show some children my shells. There are a few abandoned cars on the bridge. One burned a few months ago, the blackened husk now a favorite roost to sea-birds, pelicans mostly, judging us with their absurdly large, constipated heads. They preen their drying wings as we pass. Dorothea trades the one sea urchin we found for a large sea bass, which is fine by me.

Our house is a few blocks east of Highway Forty-One, past the high school. Some kids are up on the roof of the high school, enjoying the sunset. They wave to us and we wave back. At home, the power is still out. Dorothea and the boy go into the backyard for some limes to cut for the fish. I light candles and set the table. Some neighbors come through our house. I think I know the old man. Without the crazy, uneven beard he might have been my dentist once. The woman might be his wife. They ask for some grapefruit. I tell them we don't have any, but gesture toward the backyard, toward the lime tree. Their dirty, naked children rustle through our shells as Dorothea enters with a handful of shiny, emerald limes. One of them takes the best of the conchs and holds it to her ear. The ocean she hears must sound like the fire the boy likes to watch, the ocean Dorothea commands when she stands in the water. The dingy little girl makes me love Dorothea even more. I tell her so. She smiles and lights the stove.

The boy has fallen asleep on the couch, cradling the other dirty child. The sink in the kitchen has been giving brown water lately, so I take a pitcher into the bathroom to fill. I sit at the table waiting for dinner. The old man leaves with an armful of limes. I don't see his wife but they forgot the dirty child, leaving her with the boy in our living room.

The fish was excellent. Afterwards, we sit cross-legged on the living room floor and share slices of lotus bread. I let each slice dissolve on my tongue. As always, I feel as if I am swallowing light. Dorothea looks radiant. We touch each other with our smiles. The boy wakes up and takes some lotus bread. He is entranced by the candles on the table. He gropes for some more bread but he has already started to drool, so we don't give him any more.

Dorothea and I go into my parent's room and spread out on their bed. I lick the salt from her shoulder as she pulls down my cut-offs. The dirty child from the living room has followed us in and watches.

In the morning some people are going through our kitchen. I hope they don't take the good knives or the rest of the limes. I find some stale cereal in one of the cupboards. I listen to the portable radio. The disgusting stations rant and scream. One has beautiful music which I play loud. The people in the kitchen dance. One of them has a huge jar of lotus bread tea. They offer me a sip and I gulp it down. The boy is awake, too, so he drinks as well. His long, red hair is wild. Since he started living with us he has worn nothing but this one, long, greasy white t-shirt, like a dress. I'll have to give him some of my clothes. The people with the tea leave. Tea was a good idea so I go out into the yard to harvest the lotus bread.

Lotus bread grows at night, clutching at the morning shadows beneath any tree or shady patch, spooned across blades of grass. By noon, the lotus bread will have dried in the sun and turned to dust.

Since it's still early, the boy and I are able to gather nice, plump handfuls of the fungus. In our yard, the lotus bread comes up a dull gold, though near the beach I've seen it grow a bluish green. I've heard up north there is even red lotus bread that is spindly, like coral. I boil water for lotus bread tea for when Dorothea wakes. We will probably spend the day at the beach.

I used to listen to the people on the radio scream. When we had electricity, I used to watch them shout and debate on television. They are mad about the lotus bread. The bread came with spring. Housewives in slippers trampled it while fetching the dewy morning newspaper, kids cut through it on their bikes. On the evening news, scientists and professors were interviewed. Some called it the new kudzu, while some speculated global warming caused such changes, that this was not a new species, just newly prevalent. Was it cyclical, harmful to lawns or crops? I had done a diorama on global warming for school last year, made ice caps from Styrofoam coffee cups, so I was skeptical there. Lately I've come to believe what Dorothea has been saying all along: that the lotus bread came when we needed it most. Certainly it was not long after the appearance of the bread that someone somewhere ate a little bit. Then the answer became obvious. Lotus bread was from heaven. Ubiquitous, the mold emerges overnight wherever grass grows, hugging the greenest blades in the calmest shade. The sun dries it to powder, spreading the spores further for midnight incubation. The high is mild, peaceful. Wonderful. Children ate it off the playground; parents tenderly gathered it for morning tea. No real taste. No side effects. No addiction. Lotus bread was lotus bread, take it or leave it. Most people took to it. My parents did. They left to pick up my brother from college, packing jars of strong lotus tea in a cooler. That was a month ago and they have yet to come back. Dorothea moved in shortly after they left. She taught Latin at my high school. I was in the tenth grade but, I think she only taught seniors.

Before the electricity went, I loved to watch television. The people screaming and debating were funny. They just didn't get it. They wanted the National Guard to stop us from eating the lotus bread, and send planes to dust the towns with fungicides and poisons. Impossible, I thought. I laughed with a mouthful of lotus bread, wet crumbs bouncing off the television screen. I laughed at the picture on the news of young soldiers shooting people as they bent in their own yards, gathering their serenity, bullets exploding heads like red dandelions.

In our town, the only thing the police did was close the gas stations. They were worried too many people would drive around high. At night, the news usually showed a plane crash burning in some suburb somewhere. Before the electricity went there were lots of stories about plane crashes. By the time they closed the schools I hadn't bothered to attend for several weeks.

Now that I can't watch television, we go to the beach every day to watch the ocean. I like this more. The ocean rolls up strange treasures with one hand while eroding the sand beneath condominiums with another. Last week the rotting carcass of a giant sea turtle washed up.

We thought about dragging it back to our house to scoop out the guts from its black, octagonal shell, a perfect cauldron to brew lotus tea. The next day the sea had pulled it back out, though. I wonder, when the ocean finally knocks down one of the condominiums if another wave will come along to prop it back up, if just for a moment, a shattered resurrection, the way it gives me so many beautiful, broken shells.

The boy doesn't follow us to the beach. Dorothea and I cross the bridge, holding hands. We are barefoot and the asphalt beneath our feet is hot, scolding us for not having already made it to the shore. When the beach is in sight, we break into a run and race toward the water, laughing, past lonely parking meters and empty cars.

The water is fine. I like to hold my breath and lie underwater, close to shore. I can hear how each wave plays the bits of shell like a metallic harp, the sound of a thousand broken bones thrown against the stained glass window of an underwater cathedral. Before lotus bread, I would have waded in slowly, worried the water was too cold. Now any sense of discomfort is gone. If a mosquito bites me, I feel its needled probe slip into my skin with the same delight I feel when I slip myself into Dorothea. Everything is the same on lotus bread. Every wave-tumbled shell is a note in the symphony. Those of us who don't call it lotus bread call it Manna—Manna from Heaven, the symphony is celestial.

When I next look toward the shore, I see Dorothea fucking some man over by the parking lot. I can't really see them too well, but with his beard he looks like the old dentist who was in our house. I fish some lotus bread out of the picnic basket and place a large slice on my tongue and then go back in the water; the symphony of the day has only just begun.

Later Dorothea and the man swim next to me and we talk about tonight's bonfire. I hope someone brings another pig. Every week the neighborhood gathers for a bonfire at the high school football field. Two weeks ago someone drove up in a pick-up truck with a pig in the back. I had never seen a live pig before. They're not pink. Some boys my age killed the pig and started a smaller fire over which it was roasted. The meat was so tender and sweet, rich, better than the salt on Dorothea's brow. That was the last time I had eaten meat, not counting fish.

After swimming, we all walk up to the concession stand in the pavilion by the parking lot. I use the women's restroom with Dorothea; if I were to go into the men's room I would end up having sex all day with the men who live there. Since the man Dorothea met in the parking lot doesn't return from the restroom, we root around the concession stand on our own. Someone had pulled off the metal shutter awhile ago, so it's not really worth our efforts to look there for food. I suggest one of the hotels and Dorothea agrees. We walk past the hotels closest to the pavilion as people probably live there now. Further down the shore we walk into the lobby of one hotel. A particularly high tide must have pushed through the lobby as everything was knocked over. The stench of mildew fills the hallway. We find a vending machine and break out the glass with a chair. With a bed sheet from one of the rooms we fashion a huge sack, like Santa Claus, to drag our haul home.

Tonight there is another bonfire. We go and the boy follows us. Last week they dragged desks from classrooms to burn. Having run out of desks, people have pulled apart the bleachers. A huge pile of wood burns in the middle of the already scorched field. For some reason, older people who eat lotus bread prefer to go naked. I point this out to Dorothea and tell her I think they are uncomfortable being old. Aging must feel like wearing a heavy, itchy suit. She agrees. I recognize an old lady as the school receptionist. She's naked, save for a pearl necklace and high heels. Two naked old fat men with erections share a jar of lotus bread tea with her. The children and teenagers have started to make masks. One girl has propped the rotting skull of the last pig we cooked on her head, lopsided, like a construction worker's hard hat. Several boys have tucked tall palm fronds into improvised headbands of shoe string. They run to the fire either naked or in their underwear and throw in whatever they think will burn. Young children resurrect Halloween masks from their toy chests. The boy has taken some antlers from above my father's workbench in our garage and holds them above his head. This is quickly abandoned to the fire once he realizes that full hands means jars of lotus bread tea will pass him by.

The next day at the beach we see a submarine. It surfaces at the mouth of the bay. At first, in the distance, I think it is a whale. It hovers solidly at the surface for about an hour, a long, sleek black cylinder, impervious to the pull of the tide. The silhouettes of men appear. They walk about then disappear and the submarine submerges with a petulant blast of water. Dorothea and I think about swimming out to the sailors, bringing them some tea. I imagine they haven't had any yet. They must have put to sea two months ago, when the world was different, jagged and full of anger. They must feel so frustrated; their vessel, their shell, was built out of an umbrage that has now been erased. They must endlessly circle the seas, hoping their wake redraws the meaningless web of intrigue that defined their purpose, made their lives important. One sip of our tea would let them know life is meaningless, but agreeably so.

The boy interrupts our meditation to point out a huge fan of smoke covering the horizon behind us; possibly the reason for the sub's curiosity.

We head home then cross back over the bridge once the smoke in town gets too thick for us to see, much less breathe. There hasn't been any rain of late. The Everglades must be on fire again. This happened a few years ago. Helicopters dropped sand on the flames when they came too close to town. Now we will sleep on the beach and let the fires run their course. We manage to bring the food we found at the hotel back with us along with some lotus bread. Maybe we can go back to the same hotel and spend the night. The fire won't cross the bridge.

We walk down the beach at dusk, all the way back to the same hotel. We choose a room facing the town. The sky is a quivering orange. We feed each other wedges of the bread from our coffee can stash and stare at the sky. The orange color is low and seems to pulsate behind the flat skyline of town, a humble assortment of office buildings and hotels and meager antennas. The boy happily stayed behind, I guess to stir all of the flames with one big stick.

The hotel is hot and stuffy; the mildew smell from the lobby permeates our room. With the balcony doors open I can smell the smoke. As the lotus bread is absorbed into my bloodstream the orange in the sky throbs into a deep red. I sense a symphony coming on, one of color where occasional starlight will ring through, piercing the smoke like drums.

We lean against the rail and savor those moments when the sea breeze is stronger than the one from town, delivering a respite of rich salty air.

We had dragged the mattress out onto the balcony, so the sun on my face woke me up. The weight of Dorothea's head on my chest feels so natural. Noise from the rooms below us wakes her up. Apparently a lot of people from town followed us up the beach; the hotel appears nearly full. Some people just slept in the lobby while most others have taken over rooms. No one seems particularly concerned about town, just breakfast. On the beach, the crabs that surface from their holes to scavenge become breakfast themselves. After a daunting, leggy tap dance I catch only two, Dorothea none. I think she was laughing too hard at me to really concentrate on the crabs. A sand-smeared child proudly displays a bucket heavy with a dozen frustrated crabs. We trade the child some candy bars and cook the crabs over a fire in a wastepaper basket on our balcony. We stir up some cold instant coffee from the room's mini-bar and spread the steaming white meat over crackers. Desert, of course, is lotus bread.

After a week or so of camping out in the hotel we wander back to town. The hotel has begun to smell bad as even more people leave refuse in the lobby, piss the stairwells and shit in the pool.

In the late afternoon we cross the bridge and find a dead body. The old man who might have been my dentist is curled up in the shade of the burned out car, his face black and pulpy. Pelicans or gulls must have pecked at his eyes. The old man's leg is bent horribly. He must have fallen in the rush to leave town during the fire. I guess no one crossed the bridge those first days afterwards, leaving him to starve on the hot asphalt. That or no one bothered to help him.

Our house is as we left it. Most of the town has escaped damage; the fire must have changed course or burned out. The boy is sleeping on the kitchen floor, shirt pulled up over his face, surrounded by upturned pots and pans strewn across the linoleum. I check the radio but cannot find a station.

Tonight a large number of boys from my high school wear the shells of horseshoe crabs as masks. The gray, sharp tails point down off their chins, the barbed edges of the shell cover all but their ears and unruly hair. At the bonfire the masks make the naked teenagers servants of fire. They ferry every offering of wood to the flames as if they were delivering infants, cradling the boards and bits of furniture brought to them with a religious reverence. The heat makes their backs and buttocks slick and oily with soot and sweat, as if they had just risen from a primordial stew of reptilian essence.

The boy has taken some of my mother's lipstick and drawn crude streaks of red flame across his cheeks and forehead. He is welcomed solemnly by the older, crab-faced kids. Communal tea bowls empty quickly as everyone is thirsty from the heat of the fire. The fire is our largest yet. As it reaches out to stroke the sky, the kids behind the masks rush into the flames as one. They emerge with burning embers and march toward the high school. They set the high school on fire, throwing the burning bits of wood through some already broken windows. It takes awhile for the high school to burn. Smoldering secretly in their individual classrooms, with only hints of flame peeking from out the windows, the various small fires erupt in unison and the building begins to burn in earnest.

There is not enough lotus bread to make more tea, but everyone has some small morsel tucked away in a pocket or shoe. The boy is wild about the building burning. He keeps rushing into the building to feed more wood to the fire, though this really isn't necessary. The fire quickly grows so hot we have to watch it from across the street. There is a loud explosion from the third floor chemistry labs. The smoking bulk of an air conditioner sails over my head. The fire from the third floor changes color, from orange to pink to blue. Dorothea and I hold hands and sway with the rhythm of the flames.

The next morning the town again smells like smoke, though this time it is different. I feel a sense of pride, as if the fire we made was better than the one that burned through the Everglades. Ours was unique, a forceful stroke of a paintbrush and not the random arson of nature. The sky is gray as smoke. By the afternoon it begins to rain.

We have not had a rainstorm in weeks. Occasional light afternoon showers have kept the grass green, typical for this time of year, but nothing close to a real storm had yet come in off the ocean. At first we enjoy the rain, running through the streets, stooping to splash one another from puddles, making boats for children from whatever objects will float.

Dorothea and the boy had gathered lotus bread that morning, so after we are bored with the rain we are happy to just stay indoors and lay on the floor. It rains through the night. In the morning it is still raining with the same, steady persistence as the day before, beating a low mist off the haggard ground. No lotus bread grew during the night. What might have emerged during this deluge has surely drowned, pushed back into the soil.

The next morning I wake up and one of the horseshoe crab-faced kids is standing at the foot of our bed with a broken broomstick in his hand, rocking back and forth on his heels. He is out of breath and panting rapidly. His mask is pushed up slightly so I can see his open mouth, count his wild teeth. A dirty erection parts the tatters of his loin cloth. He looks at me then Dorothea then turns and leaves.

I put a plastic garbage bag over the top of my head and go out to search the yard for lotus bread. I look up and down my street and see several other desperate figures similarly squatting in their yards in the rain.

I wake Dorothea and tell her I couldn't gather any bread and she just smiles. She reminds me that before the big fire she had placed water and lotus bread in empty soda bottles, sealed them and placed them in the rafters of the attic above our bedroom. Her idea was that after the lotus bread dissolved into the water we should let it sit and ferment, hopefully increasing the tea's potency.

I stand on the bed and swat at the attic's trap door pulley until I catch it. Retrieving one of the three soda bottles we sit on the bed and sample our new, dark and muddy brew. The boy climbs into bed with us and we all take long swigs from the soda bottle. The taste is thicker, almost sweet, and the effect immediate and strong. A flood of warmth spreads over us. We feel, in unison, as if our bed is stamped by God to be his special place, a place where no sound is necessary, no movement.

Everything is understood.

☺

Later, as this wonderment slowly falls away, I realize night has fallen and people are searching our house. Dorothea follows me into the living room to find a group of people going through our kitchen cabinets. It is dark and they have flashlights. Someone had taken our candles. The beams from the flashlights bounce around the room, reflecting crazy nebulas off the pots on the floor. The men and women are wearing more clothes than I've seen on anyone in a long time, pensive expressions screwed on their faces. They have been without lotus bread for at least a day. Clearly they don't crave it, they *miss* it.

Once they realize we are home they rush out without a word. Embarrassment, another sign they are without the bread. Dorothea and I look at each other in the dark. We decide to go to our neighbors homes and see if they have candles. We go from house to house and find the same thing: confused, nervous people. Our closest neighbor is pushing a dead vacuum cleaner around a dark dining room as we walk in the door. She screams when she realizes people are in her house, *strangers*. People have not been strangers since the bread came. Dorothea laughs at the horrible face fear puts on the woman and screams back at her.

House after house we find people who did not know what to do without the bread. Someone drives past us in a mad race up the street. I haven't seen someone drive a car in weeks. At the next house we finally find one smart man who had begun to drink some all-but-forgotten whiskey. He is drunk enough to let us into his home as if it were natural. Loud Southern Rock blares from a small portable tape player perched like a seesaw across his large stomach. He doesn't care that we take some candles and even offers us a drink. *Tastes better than rain,* he laughs, raising a shot glass and knocking over the stereo.

By the time we make it back to our own dark house we are soaked, shaken and badly in need of lotus bread tea. I light the candles so we can see. The boy is sprawled on the bed, arms out, the other two soda bottles empty at his bare, blackened feet. I grab one of the bottles and hold it above my lips. Not a drop left. I leap wildly for the cord to the attic door. Searching the attic for another bottle, knowing there were only three, I jump back down onto the bed, defeated, wet and cold. I watch the boy. He purrs in his sleep, the R.E.M. beneath his eyelids a metronome of bliss. So much bread races though his little body his jugular visibly thumps. Dorothea is one thought ahead of me.

She returns from the kitchen with two large carving knives. While I carry him to the bathtub she puts her hair in a bun, never taking her eyes off the boy. I can't find a stopper for the drain so I twist his filthy shirt into the black hole. Dorothea has already made the initial cut at the boy's neck. With her finger she brings a drop of blood to her tongue. The boy tightens his shut eyes in an angry squint and purrs louder, an insolent noise, as if his great sleep might be wrongly interrupted.

Dorothea is still for a moment. Eyes closed she rocks back and forth slightly, this from one drop. Shuddering with anticipation I widen the dark, plum hole in his neck with my finger and drink. Hot wine gushes from his neck, his neck a fountain around which the world will surely dance.

SICK DAYS

Madge pulled the van into the driveway and sat behind the wheel. The other lawns and homes were too clean; the yards' neat, virginal turf seemed artificial. No bikes crossed sidewalks, no stationary balls impressing brown fingerprints of dead grass. The Marshals across the street had disassembled the swing set they had bought their children. Ron Marshal had stayed home one day and taken it down while everyone was at work. They were like that, thoughtful and discreet.

Madge felt a pang in her chest as she removed the keys from the ignition. Dusk was settling a fine, brassy hue across the tree-line that protected their sharp little development from the expressway. The leaves were thinning with fall. She could see the grey boards of the tree-house behind the Canes' place. Their home was dark. Various neighbors haphazardly took turns mowing their yard but it still showed neglect. They had left two months ago. When kids first started getting sick they took their children and moved in the middle of the night. No calls, no forwarding address, nothing. Madge imagined them grimly packing in the night, driving off at dawn, stopping for donuts and coffee, content in their decision, smug even, as if they were abandoning a sinking ship when really, the whole of the ocean tossed and churned and parents everywhere felt as if they were drowning. She tried to remember the boys' names; she and her husband Bob were never close to the Canes, but trying to recall the names of their children deepened the invisible wound in her chest. Wearily, she got out of the van and pushed such thoughts out of her mind. It was Bob's turn to cook dinner, and she reminded herself not to criticize his meatloaf. She was always after his cooking. *Meatloaf is meatloaf,* she thought, smiling, smiling for the first time all day. She fixed the look tightly on her face, hoping to erase the creeping, undefined doubt that lately was her more usual expression.

From the driveway she could tell all of the lights were on in the house. That was his thing, leaving all of the lights on. She knew that inside the kids were watching a movie. The television was always on these days, but no matter what movie was playing. No news. They were reminded of the outside world enough. The time to watch the news was after the children had been put to bed, and then only in their room, with the door closed and the volume low. Even then, she did not want to watch, but of course you had to, it was all anyone talked about at the office, always ending their conversation with the same wistful phrase, *You're so lucky.* And not always wistful, sometimes there was an edge of anger, jealousy, and then embarrassment, though not that many people talked to her at work anymore, with certain, noted exceptions. That was fine. *Work is work,* Madge told herself. And opening the front door, her presence was known to all. The twins leapt up from before the TV and rushed to embrace her. Bob gave a booming salutation, and the depth and the richness of his voice still surprised her after all these years. Appearing momentarily, waving hands comically swallowed by massive blue oven mitts, the tips of each freshly burned, he quickly disappeared back into the kitchen. The children crushed against her legs, warming her. She dropped quickly to give them each a kiss, catching herself as she started to feel their foreheads for fever, with the superstition that such constant precaution might somehow be *inviting.*

For the last few months they ate around the dining room table, something they had never done before. "My mom would die if she could see this," Bob said, his mouth half-full with mashed potatoes. Frances was stirring her fork in hers, making a circle. She never seemed to eat, while Natalie ate dutifully and quietly, stopping only to smile at her Dad, who was an endless source of funny faces and bold pronouncements. The dinners around the table were grand. Frances pushed her peas into the center of the mashed potatoes, stopping to admire her masterpiece before stabbing at the bit of lamb still on her plate. Every time Madge looked away Bob would steal a piece of her lamb. She would giggle slightly, thrilled at the conspiracy. Madge pretended to be clueless. Moments like this made the levity seem real. It was important to keep the children happy, and the best way to do that was to pretend they were happy, and in pretending for so long, it had begun to feel real.

The slice of lamb in Madge's mouth turned heavy, tasteless. *I am enjoying myself,* she thought. *Since we started having dinner together I've loved every fucking minute of it.* They used to eat in the living room watching CNN after the kids had eaten in the kitchen, or in the family room, two TV's blaring. She caught Bob looking at her and forced a smile back at him. He had detected the subtle shift in her, he always did, in the same way he monitored the girls, laughing, teasing, but always ready to swoop down and save them from a fall, inspect a boo-boo or tie a dirty pink shoe lace. He nodded reassuringly to her as Skippy came bounding down the steps to beg for scraps. Skippy had been Bob's idea, too. A furry ball of energy, a total mutt, shaggy hair, black skid-marks beneath tearful eyes—the girls adored him. Madge had never liked dogs, had had two cats in fact, both still at her mother's. Bob had an allergy she had always suspected to be half-feigned. But the day she came home from a horrible, horrible day at the office, where she realized she was the only woman who had made it in to work. The only woman surrounded by men unshaven, or wearing the same shirt and tie they had on the day before, listless men, all of the women home. Those who were mothers were home with their sick children, and those who were not all happened to be out at the same time, most likely attending funerals. She had almost quit that day. But instead had come home to Skippy and the children jumping up and down on the couch as the dog barked happily. She'd fully joined in their frenzy, dizzily rushing each end of the couch as the girls shrieked louder seeing Mommy, knowing she would be surprised. And she was. Bob lay nearby on the carpet, smiling broadly. *We might just make it*, she thought, squatting down by her husband to pick fur off his pants. *We just might make it. This man is going to hold us together.*

She rose quickly from the dinner table to rush upstairs. Running the shower she cried in the bathroom. Exhausted, heaving, she sat on the toilet as she had done for nearly a month and cried, but this was the first time she cried in relief, not desperation.

After they put the girls to bed they hurriedly undressed. Though more frequent than even during college, their fucking now lacked rhythm; it wasn't rushed, but it felt like something that had to be done. Every connection had to be made. She hated it when Skippy would scratch at the door while they were doing it, but Bob would not put him in the garage. He wanted Skippy in the house, on call for the girls twenty-four hours a day. *He's really circling the wagons*, she thought, lying atop the bed while he showered. She heard the water go off then she entered the bathroom, kissing him in passing, his lips hot from the water, his meaty chest brushing her shoulder. He had gained a lot of weight since he started working from home. *Maybe for Christmas I'll get him one of those jogging machines.* She stepped onto the scale. *No, he'll want me to use it, too.*

Bob turned on his computer while Madge pulled out of the drive. He wanted to log-on and answer a few e-mails early on, to show everyone at the office he was getting an early start—that he was indeed on the job. He logged-on and sent a snarly e-mail to Human

Resources about the latest snafu, carbon copying his bosses. He parked the girls in front of the TV and told them they could watch a *Scooby Doo* movie, but after that they had to walk the dog with him and do some math.

Upstairs he gathered towels and clothes from the hamper. He was glad Madge took a shower every night when she came home. She used to only shower in the mornings. He was glad she was taking precautions, but she still forgot to leave her shoes outside like he had gently asked so many times. It would be nice if she could take a shower first, before hugging the kids, but he just hadn't thought of the right way to ask her. He took the laundry basket to the kitchen, kicking some blocks out of the way. The girls were enraptured with Scooby Doo. It was all he could do to keep them from naming the dog Scooby Doo; it seemed too obvious, though at the time he didn't know their second choice would be Skippy, as in their favorite peanut butter. Having already stepped more than once in one of the little nasty surprises Skippy had left on the carpet, Bob found the name rather apt. While loading the washer, the doorbell rang.

Madge came home and Skippy was excitedly at her ankles, but the TV was off. "Honey?" she called, dropping her purse, ready to race back out to the van, imagining the time it would take to drive to the hospital with rush hour traffic. Bob called out from the kitchen, "We're in here."

We? Fuck this. "Where are the girls?" Madge did not bother to conceal the stridency in her voice.

"Upstairs, upstairs, coloring in their room," Bob emerged from the kitchen, a beer in hand. *That's different,* Madge thought. She hadn't had a beer in ages, and the brown, sweaty bottle looked inviting. From over Bob's shoulder Ron Marshal stepped forward, ashen and disheveled. "It's Wendy, Madge, she left," he said.

"Oh Christ, Ron, I'm sorry." She hugged him, looking over his shoulder at Bob, her eyes wide.

He misinterpreted her look as one of anger and shrugged, but Bob was prescient enough to have reached for another beer from the fridge. Popping the cap, he handed it to her. She gave Ron another squeeze and pulled away; taking the bottle from her husband she shook her head, sorry not that he misread her anger, but sorry that every time she met someone she ended up apologizing or offering condolences. She withdrew, always wondering when the next opportunity would present itself for her to wash her hands.

The horrible thing was that Madge had thought Wendy would leave. She and Ron were so mismatched—Wendy was wild, carefree to the brink of disaster, while Ron was as calm and mild as a man could be. Wendy had picked up on this observation from Madge early on in their friendship and whispered in an aside, "You marry the one who will be a good father, not a good lay. Ron's both, of course, sure, but in college I had to teach him everything. I had to teach him how to drink. But Madge, I'll tell you, he was the only kid in school watching the stock market, and I wasn't the only girl watching him."

Not exactly an impressive sentiment, Madge thought at the time, but the Marshals had the biggest house in the development, and their combination of parental styles had produced two wonderful children, quick friends for Frances and Natalie, a boy and a girl nearly the same age. All four had the most angelic blonde hair. They could have been siblings.

They used to carpool together before the schools were closed. The Marshal's children were the first in the neighborhood to get sick. She had left the men in the kitchen and gone upstairs to shower. Another swig of her beer and she felt calm, level. She looked in on the girls who were quietly coloring in their room. *This home schooling thing was not working. Another month of Bob's teaching methods, they're going to forget they ever knew the alphabet.* She was glad the girls didn't see her at the door; she did not want to answer questions about Ron, or where the Marshal kids were. *They're in heaven, honey.*

She imagined her answer, starting the shower and letting her clothes fall on the floor.

As the mirror slowly steamed she pulled at her auburn hair. It was too long, had too many split ends. *They're in the ground, honey, and their parents are losing their minds. Now, can you tell me your ABC's?* And then she broke her promise. She had promised herself not to cry tonight. Every night she made this promise not to cry. *Through sickness and in health.* She stepped into the too hot water, hoping to feel cleansed.

Later, she put the girls in her and Bob's room, to watch a movie, telling them to camp out on Mommy and Daddy's bed while the grown-ups had dinner. The girls took to the idea like it was an adventure; Bob had even come up with some of the pillows from the couch, fashioning a rather precarious fort. And Ron, always proper, warm but formal, did not cry. *I knew he wouldn't. The bastard.* He sat there blinking behind thick glasses. His jaw was square enough to be considered masculine, but his neck was too thin. And he was wearing a red flannel shirt that was too new and stiff, so that even out of his suit he still seemed overdressed, artificial. Madge knew to stop after the second beer, but she wanted to grab him by the shoulders and shake him, tell him to cry. *Cry damn it, fucking cry!*

She had seen him weep mildly at the joint funeral for his children. Wendy had cried; she had really lost it, clung to the caskets as her parents and Ron tried to pull her away. And Bob had cried, so loudly and openly it had startled Madge into a self-conscious silence. She had never seen her husband cry before. He was not meant to cry. She was mad, as if he took her emotions and used them before she had a chance, but his cheeks were so swollen, his open mouth gulping at air. She could only hug him, squeeze herself into his chest and hide her dry face in the arm of his blazer. He held her, his touch sure as gravity, yet she was so scared. They were the only parents from the neighborhood to attend the funeral, and she had not wanted them to go. But so many other parents were tending to sick children, or were afraid of the Marshals and had stayed away; so *they* had to go. Their girls were fine. Home with their grandmother, Bob's mother graciously flying in on the red-eye from Florida to watch them and help out around the house. To prepare.

Over that weekend school closings would be announced. Even without the closings, no sane parent would take their children to school that coming week. Everyone was staying home, watching the news and avoiding each other. That first week was the hardest. Horrors visited every house. Any adult who sneezed was banished to a hotel, beaten, and forced out of their homes by a husband or wife. Then a rumor swept the country that pets carried the disease, and pets were pushed out, family dogs dropped off out by the dump, doggie doors boarded up. She heard barking one night that second week, and then two shots, a car alarm startled to life by the vibrations, then silence.

The Kelly's next door to the Marshals had sick children.

So too, did the Chutes, a boy and a girl. All of them stayed at home now. Not long after the Marshal children died, the Kellys brought their children home. Madge was horrified that they wouldn't want to keep them in the hospital. But the hospitals were full. And as this epidemic played out, that was the coming trend. To store your sick at home. Madge had seen a commercial for a bed guard, to keep "those still sleeping" from rolling out of bed at night. The phrase sickened her.

Shortly after that, their neighbors and colleagues at work all started to say the same thing. *You are so lucky.* Yes, their girls were fine, they shone like healthy angels, while everyone else's kids were withered and fevered and comatose. *I feel lucky,* Madge had wanted to say, *Lucky to kiss them good night on their foreheads, wondering if I'm putting them to bed or taking their temperature. Lucky to lie to them. Telling my children their friends are at their grandparents' houses. That school is closed because they are painting the building! How Bob guffawed at that one. I couldn't think of anything better to say, but he's different, his relationship with them is. He spends all day with them, in their little private world. I spend my days with depressed co-workers.* Still, Bob had already been working from home quite a lot. He had been with his company for years, they had relocated for them; he was senior management. He still had to go in occasionally. When he did she would use a sick day to stay home, grateful for the private time it afforded her with the girls. To just sit and watch them…it felt like a luxury. She was running out of sick days, vacation days and personal days. She wished they had never taken that vacation to Lake George, before the whole thing started. She used up a lot of time and they had spent a lot of money. Ron had been helpful, after the epidemic had begun. They had gone to the Marshals for dinner and he had rightly guessed that she would want to quit her job. He recommended she stay on until she was let go- that companies would be down-sizing in the final quarter; they discussed that her position might not be as strong as Bob's—she worked in marketing, he was the head of an IT team for a fiscally conservative company; he would be fine. Ron recommended they both reduce the amount of money they put into their 401k's and start saving as much as possible.

After dinner, at the door, Wendy gave them a bag of new clothing for the girls. It was all un-worn, brand new. *It had been in my truck the whole time, I just kept forgetting to bring them in,* she said. This was her way of telling Madge the clothes were uncontaminated, good. They accepted the gift without hesitation; Madge brought the bag to the office with her the next day and threw it in the rusted green dumpster behind the parking lot.

After Ron had left, Bob helped Madge carry the girls to bed, each taking a limp body from their room. He pushed the cushions to the floor, both of them too tired and a bit buzzed from the beer for the usual frenzied sex. Madge was both annoyed and grateful Bob had started to cum so fast. *Maybe being around the girls all day he doesn't get to masturbate any more.* He turned on the TV while she struggled into her nightgown. Of course they watched the news. The newscaster sat before a glowing map of the United States and

Canada. All of the states and provinces were now pink or deeply red to indicate infection levels.

The epidemic came at the end of summer, the start of school, was seemingly everywhere, but most virulently in California and the Eastern Seaboard, before it spread rapidly, reaching toward itself to consume a continent. The red states were fully infected, while the pink states were still rising. In the news: Florida a healthy child was kidnapped by gunpoint at a pharmacy, a grieving parent replacing a lost child. They showed a large picture of a shy little girl with cherry barrettes pinning back a mass of black hair. Congress voted to extend unemployment benefits another six months for parents who had lost their jobs or were forced to stay home and tend to sick, comatose children. The dollar weakened further against the yen. Every country was struck by the epidemic, but the workforce in the U.S. seemed more traumatized; a professorial looking type told the newscaster this likely had to do with cultural differences. More elderly lived with their children in Asian countries, and were on hand to help nurture the sick. Europeans had more vacation days. The news cut to a scene of a hospital burning in Spain, a riot over an antibiotic shortage.

Bob hit the mute button and turned to Madge. "I need to be in the office Monday."

She hated that he never asked that she take a day off, or what her schedule was, just announced his. "Well Bob, it's the end of the month. We're pulling ads like crazy and it's just killing our venders…I mean, I'll see who else is in." Meaning of course she would do it and be at home. She had to check how many sick days she had left, and if she was allowed to take unpaid leave. With that, he turned off the TV and they lay there in the darkness, silently waiting for sleep to overtake them.

At work, a woman was crying in the break room. Madge was furious with herself for being so annoyed with the woman, but she wanted a cup of coffee and did not want to interrupt the woman's privacy. Really she did not want to put herself in the position where she would have to console the poor woman. She imagined herself offering a hug and again being told how "lucky" she was. That word made her want to scream. *We should have named the dog Lucky.* Going back to her desk she grabbed her coat and went out to the strip mall across the street. She grabbed a coffee at Starbucks and called Bob from her cell phone.

"I'm out of sick days, Bob."

Pause. "Then I won't go in."

She ran her free hand through her knotted hair. "Wait," she said. "What about your mother?" "She's at Nancy's." Silence.

Madge knew she was at Nancy's. She had been at Nancy's since her little girl got sick. They understood that Nancy was in trouble. She was a single mother who rashly quit her job the day her daughter went into the hospital. Bob's mother had flown from their house straight to Nancy's to help her cope with a sick child, now home, on a ventilator in the living room: her tiny nursery was too small for the hospital bed and machinery that was rented out at an exorbitant fee from a local nursing home. Nancy had refused to take their calls; she was nakedly hostile to both of them, hating them for having healthy children. More than once Madge had begrudgingly admired the honesty of Nancy's attitude. When Wendy gave her those clothes Madge had felt like she had been handed a bag of explosives; at least Nancy refused to talk to them. Really, it was a relief. Except for Bob's mother, who was more than annoyed by her only daughter's growing Evangelical streak.

"Bob, I have one vacation day left and I was saving it for the Friday after Thanksgiving. I'll use that. Just remember, I wasn't the one who wanted to go to the fucking lake." She hung up. Looking at her reflection in the dirty windowpane of Starbucks, she thought how she hated her khaki winter coat, long and worn, khaki; it hung crooked on her shoulders. She looked like some cheap caricature of a private detective. *When I quit this job, I'll burn this coat. And we could sell one of the cars.* She thought about selling the van. It wasn't that old and they didn't carpool anymore.

When she pulled into their street she saw Ron walking, down past the Chutes' house. She was about to honk and pull up beside him, but he was clutching something odd. She idled at the intersection leading toward their street and peered at him; Ron was carrying an ax. She drove up slowly toward their drive, her van matching his pace. As she pulled into their driveway she watched Ron walk across the Canes' shaggy yard and behind their house. The trees had continued to thin until the low tree house loomed large against the orange skyline of the setting sun.

As she turned the key in the front door she heard the deadening "thwack" of ax hitting wood. Once the kids were settled at the table for dinner, she pulled Bob into the kitchen and told him what she saw.

"I guess I should stop taking the girls with me when I walk the dog," he said. He held her from behind while she stirred the vegetables, turning the heat down low, covering the pot to let them simmer in their own juices.

After dinner they had a few beers. Bob gently reminded her to leave her shoes outside. She asked him just how much money he planned to spend every month. Since he had been working from home he had bought the dog, a new TV and mail-ordered a ton of DVD's. "The dog's therapeutic," he replied, giving her a beery, sloppy kiss. They fucked, this time not so fast, the alcohol fueling them, adding a touch of provocation; they did it in the laundry room, Skippy shut upstairs with the girls. The phone rang sometime after ten but they let the machine get it. Whoever it was hung up. Caller ID showed a local number neither of them could identify.

Madge woke up feeling out of sorts, heavy. She wondered if her period was early when, mildly surprised, she realized she was hung-over. It had been a long time. While the coffee was brewing she leaned her forehead against the cool refrigerator door; she hated that it was Friday. She looked forward to her time with the girls this coming Monday: it was an opportunity to get them back on track with their addition and subtraction. She had read an article that had some great suggestions on how to make it more like a game. It was the coming weekend she dreaded. The weekends were the hardest. With the four of them home, the twins got worked up and wanted to go outside.

Saturday the girls came bursting into their room. Frances made the bed in a single leap and jumped up and down on the mattress, shifting the hills of comforter and pillow. Bob didn't stir, and Madge groped for the clock: 6:30 AM. "Girls, watch cartoons. Mommy needs to sleep."

In unison: "We want to go to the playground! We want to go to the playground!"

"Okay, okay, we'll see. Go watch cartoons." Frances withdrew from the bed.

As she closed the door Natalie whispered, "If Peter and Maggie are back, let's bring them, too."

Peter and Maggie. The Marshal children. Madge lay there, wide awake, not knowing what to do.

Bob walked down the drive to retrieve the paper while Skippy did his business underneath the lone pine tree centered in the yard. Jimmy Chute was jogging by. *Christ*, Bob thought. *What do I have to do, peek out the window every time I step outside?* He stooped to pick up the paper, giving a wave toward Jimmy with his other arm. Jimmy did the marathon every year. Now when he jogged he pushed a giant carriage, his drooling, comatose children strapped in. He stopped in front of their house and bent over to grab his knees, breathing heavy. Jimmy Jr.'s head lolled about; he and Jessie were dressed in matching jumpsuits. They looked like they had just dozed off, each taking a little nap from which they soon would awaken. Bob noticed Jimmy was looking up at him. Jimmy straightened, kicked one leg in the air, caught it and stretched. Bob hated the shorts Jimmy always wore. There was something obscene about the excessive slit running shorts had these days; too much thigh from a middle-aged man was never a good thing.

Panting, Jimmy said, "Jes-Jessie. Moved. Moved her finger last night. Good sign."

"Yeah?" Bob replied, trying to sound encouraging, wishing, just for once, Madge would get the paper in the morning. At least on the weekend, it was the least she could do.

Jimmy felt his sweaty neck, taking his own pulse. "I like them to get fresh air." He spat the words at Bob, who could only say, "Of course, of course." Saliva had hardened into a white crust in the corners of Jimmy Jr.'s mouth, which hung open like a battered mailbox.

Bob rubbed his arms, pretending to be cold, and said, "Well, I better get back inside."

Jimmy was already jogging off, pushing the stroller, when he shot back, "Hey. Keep an eye on Ron. He seems a little down."

Bob already had one hand on the doorknob. He shouted back, "Sure. Will do."

Madge was making peanut butter sandwiches for lunch, thinking about the call tree from school. They were given the numbers of the other parents in Frances' and Natalie's class. They had pretty much laughed it off; everyone in their neighborhood had kids around the same age, at the same school, except the Canes, who sent their kids to Temple. It was great that the girls played so well together. She had read horror stories about siblings so close in age. Still, she knew they missed their friends; they had yet to sense something was wrong, but really, one of them was bound to ask just how long it took to paint a school. They asked pretty regularly about the Marshal kids.

She put the jelly back in the fridge and wondered where they put the phone tree list. What was she going to do, anyway? Actually call these people? *Hi, you don't know me, but my daughters went to*

Strickland Elementary with your son/daughter... I was wondering if they were still alive? If they're not comatose, would you like to arrange a play date? Before shutting the refrigerator door she grabbed herself a beer.

It was hard, not taking the kids to the playground. Every excuse was different: it was too cold, it might rain, Daddy had a headache. Bob actually thought it would be okay, that likely no other children would be there. But Madge just did not want to them to go. The sickness was probably spread like the common cold, through children's hands and children's coughs. It had come on so fast, though. And so thoroughly. Madge felt as if it were an *unnatural disaster*. Nothing biblical, like her sad, sad sister-law insisted.

Bob's mother had confided to her that Nancy spent most of the day at church, leaving her alone with a bedridden child, forcing her to lengthen her stay indefinitely. Madge knew she missed the twins, missed a living household. Still, she felt horrible that she didn't try to call Nancy, but with the epidemic came a new sense of isolation. They were the survivors; Madge did not feel superior: she felt scared. She had felt scared for her children's safety since the onset of the disease. Seeing Ron walk down the street with an ax, her dread had widened to encompass concerns she could not yet articulate. She knew one thing: it was time Bob bought a gun.

Helen Chute came over that afternoon. Madge was always closer to Wendy, which surprised her. Not really *close*, per se, but Wendy was fun. You never knew what she was going to say. You always knew what Helen was going to say. She was going to talk about her kids. Every parent did; certainly she and Bob doted. But Helen had a way of discussing her children as if they were an on-going project integral to Society's Evolution: their greatness was assured. Worse, she and Jimmy were both psychologists, and both of them spoke in such measured terms, everything so appropriate, *deliberate,* it left her cold. Madge really didn't want anyone in her house, but her guilt and curiosity let Helen get as far as the kitchen.

While two cups of water heated in the microwave, she foraged in the cabinet for tea. Helen sat poised on a stool by the counter, looking out toward the living room. Madge sat close to her and whispered, "We haven't told them anything," giving Helen a stern look.

If she was going to offer professional advice on honesty and disclosure, Madge didn't want to hear it. Helen fingered her hair. It was perfect as always—strawberry blonde, certainly off the shelf, she and Wendy had long ago decided. *With all of their trouble, she has time to get her hair done and I don't,* Madge thought, standing as the microwave beeped. She returned with two steaming mugs.

Helen smiled: "Well, I'm pregnant," her head tilted, awaiting Madge's response. Madge was beyond stunned. Something like anger had to be swallowed before she could stammer out an acceptable follow-up to mask her sudden discomfort.

"How far along are you?"

"Three weeks. I know it's soon, but I wanted to tell someone. I mean you." *Again the smile. Only a psycho would tell someone, a neighbor, this early.*

"Have you told Jimmy?" She blew on her tea.

"Of course, Madge," Helen said frostily. "This was something we *planned.*"

Well certainly, everything they did was planned.

"So you aren't, aren't…." Madge had wanted to ask her about her practice as a child psychologist, but surely that had dried up, this being a city of sleeping children. A world of sleeping children. *Nap-time everybody. Lights out.* Madge recalled that babies born after the onset of the epidemic had caught it in a matter of days. That young, many of them could not withstand the fever, and mostly died.

Helen ignored the unfinished question. "Jimmy and I talked about it. I'm thirty-five and I might as well maximize my time and have another baby. Jimmy's practice is doing so well right now."

Madge smiled. *Maximize your time? That's something you do when you pick up your dry cleaning on the way to the grocery store.* But Helen was not looking at her but watching the living room. *She's waiting for the girls to come down. She wants to see what living children look like.* Madge regretted the thought and, not knowing what to say, gulped her tea. Helen hadn't touched hers. Mustering all of the goodwill she could, from the depths of her weary soul, Madge smiled and said, "You guys must be so excited. Are you going to turn Jimmy's office into a nursery?"

"We have the spare bedroom for that. We've always wanted a large family." At that, the girls came rambling down the stairs, screeching Helen's name. They rushed into the kitchen and Helen bent to hug them both. Madge leapt to get the cookie tin out of the pantry; armed with sweets, she could get them into the living room and away from Helen, who looked up at her.

"Actually, they're why I am here. Now that I'm definitely going to be home full-time, I wanted you to know I'd be happy to baby-sit."

"That would be great," Madge said, too loudly. "I can't wait to tell Bob."

"Great. That's great. And Jessie moved a finger yesterday."

Weekends, they were prisoners in their own home. Still, they made the weekend as enjoyable as possible: Bob on all fours, barreling through their living room fort of sheets and pillows. Bob sleeping on the couch while she and the girls sat in her sewing room and cut and pasted. It was too early for Christmas, but they cut out Christmas trees from green cardboard and drew on ornaments. The girls wanted McDonalds but Madge told them they were having their *other* favorite, macaroni and cheese.

At least they had the coming winter as an excuse to stay indoors. Spring would be a real problem, if it lasted until spring. There was that hope. Hope remained. Madge did not like taking the children with her anywhere in the car; secretly she feared she would have an accident and the girls would be killed. She would survive and have to tell Bob that in the middle of a horrific plague she had coasted through a red light while trying to find a radio station and killed their daughters. That and the contagion. The epidemic seemed to be spread by other children, and sick adults, so no park, no McDonalds. The disease was like mild influenza in adults and in older teenagers. It hit small children like a cinderblock. Except their children. And others—not every child came down with this ruinous flu. Just every child they knew.

They were both in bed, sharing a beer, watching the news. "Let's move." Madge handed him the bottle.

"Honey. These things are cyclical." Bob took a swig and uncrossed his feet, sinking lower into the bed.

"Sure. Like that's what Europeans must have said about the Black Death. It's fucking cyclical. That or God hates us." She grabbed at the bottle but he held it over the edge of the bed.

"Okay. Where do you want to go?" He sounded like he meant it, so she sat up.

"Anywhere. Away from this neighborhood. I can't believe Helen's having a baby."

He took a long pull from the beer, finishing it. "Amy at the office is pregnant."

She shot up. "What? Why didn't you say anything?" He shrugged, staring at the TV.

"It seems…it seems so morbid. I guess they're trying to fill the void. The grief. Hoping it will all be over in a couple of months." He looked at her with bloodshot eyes.

"And if it isn't? Well, at least they'll never be woken up by babies' crying! They'll have these sleeping infants. I'm freaked out by Jimmy's stroller, Bob. Pushing around that drooling kid. I'm freaked out by fucking Ron, Bob. I want friends. I want to get out of here so bad." Before she could say another word he put his hands to his face and started to weep. So she shut up. Furious that she wanted to cry and he would interrupt her, rob her of her anger. Again. She patted his head then started smoothing out the strands, thinking he looked thin on top again. He was forgetting his Rogaine. She'll put the bottle out by the sink in the morning to remind him. This was the first time he had cried since the funeral. Her anger gave way to sadness. The fear inside her was gaining definition. She'll ask about the gun another night.

Bob stood in the meeting room and talked about the network. Really he threw information around more than talked, giving a long stream of facts, never mentioning costs. It was the final quarter and the big boys never wanted to hear about costs. *Let them think this is all going to pay for itself, I don't care. As long as I don't have to fly to Washington to tell headquarters. I can't be away from the girls right now, and Madge seems tender.* He stopped and looked at the phone in the middle of the table. It was silent. "Are you guys still there?"

Pause and crackle. A robotic "yes" emanated from the speaker. "Okay. Thought we lost you. Any questions?"

"Yeah," from the phone, "How much is this going to cost?"

Bob went to Applebee's with senior staff for lunch. This was fine; not only was he showing his face around the office but this gave him a chance to hear what the old guys thought. Brenda, the Vice President of Marketing was a lesbian, and had no kids. Chuck, the CEO, and his wife, their children were grown. Rob, the CFO, was an ancient eunuch. Gary the Project Manager had a little boy who was sick and was not in the office today. Brenda complained about her staff; she always did. Chuck looked serene, his white hair plastered back; he had a great, knowing smile but you could never really see what was in his eyes. Everyone waited to see if he would order a scotch after lunch. He did, so everyone got a beer or whiskey. Brenda pushed brown hair out of her eyes. Having tanned skin, and always wearing a brown suit, Bob thought of her as a somewhat disgruntled teddy bear. Rob was practically a corpse. He didn't come alive until he had a drink.

Thank God Chuck ordered. And Rob always gets the same thing as Chuck, no matter what. Sycophant. Bob took a small sip from his drink. *You don't want to get too loose with this crew.*

"So where's Garry?" The moment he asked, Bob realized he had made a mistake. Brenda just looked at him. Rob made a strange noise from somewhere in his chest. Chuck stopped smiling.

"We don't know, Bob. I was going to say something about it right now. I just wanted to finish lunch. I didn't want to throw you off before the phone call with Washington and all."

"I don't get it." Bob looked into his drink, possibilities flooding his mind.

"Neither do we. Gary didn't come to work last Monday. His assistant called the house and his wife said he left for the office at the usual time. Of course our call upset her. Home alone with the boy and all. Well, he didn't go home that night. Nobody's seen him since."

"God," Bob uttered, finishing his whiskey and waving the waiter over. He ordered another round. Everyone seemed to exhale at once.

"She's called the police, of course, and filled out a missing person's report. You know how dejected he's been since…." Chuck let his words trail off. He stared past Bob's shoulder into an undefined nothingness, the slow sifting shine of the lights off the brass railing that surrounded their booth. Brenda cleared her throat. "We haven't said anything to the office. I mean, Thanksgiving's coming up. And there's already been so much…"

"God," Bob repeated. Chuck nodded his head, took a drink and refocused his gaze on the grey eunuch, Rob.

"Rob, if this turns into a *thing*, make sure HR doesn't cut his paycheck off until the last possible minute. His wife will need the money. Life insurance doesn't pay out for suicide. Bob, send an e-mail that Gary's taken a leave of absence."

Bob sat there, struggling to remember the name of Gary's wife.

That night, in the kitchen, he confided to his wife that he thought they were going to fire him. Madge poked at the steaks frying in the skillet with a long, two-pronged fork. "Bob, that's crazy. You're just being paranoid."

"Sure. They just forgot to mention that one of the senior staff wandered off and never came back." He took a pull from his beer.

"Listen," she said. The steaks were done and she wished he would set the table rather than just stand there. "Rob's got problems. Everyone there's got problems. Not telling you doesn't mean you're out of the loop or something." She sighed and reached for the dinner plates, letting the steaks darken in the pan. He took the plates from her and rushed them to the table, where vegetables were already cooling in a white dish.

"Girls!" they both yelled in tandem, and then laughed.

"Remember when you wanted to buy that place at the lake?"

Frances twisted in her blue pajamas; she could never get the top on right. Bob kneeled down and gave Natalie an Eskimo kiss. She giggled lightly as their noses touched. "Sure. You hated the idea."

Frances, finally done, leapt into bed. Madge smelled shampoo in her hair as she kissed her good night. They passed each other as they crossed the room to kiss the other waiting child good night, their dual presence invisibly interlocking, like the crossing of wakes. Madge always felt that moment each night, as the center point to their lives. Bob turned off the light and she followed him out.

Shutting the door to their room, he asked why she mentioned the lake.

"I don't know. We should leave. We should buy a place in the woods, cash in our 401k's and just wait this out." She looked at him. He could tell she didn't mean it.

"And do what? Live off the land? I'm not Grizzly Adams, honey. I don't even know how to fish." He sat on the bed and pulled off his socks.

She sat next to him and put her head on his shoulder. "Then maybe we should go to your Mom's house for a little while. The girls love Florida—the weather's great this time of year. We just need to do *something*." Bob thought about it, turned on the TV, and settled back into the pile of pillows.

When Madge came home, the front door was slightly ajar. She pushed the door inward with her extended key and called Bob's name.

"We're in here, honey." *We,* she thought.

He'd left the door open on purpose. *He's trying to warn me.* She stood there. *Does he want me to run? Where are the girls?* "Bob, come here. I need some help." She said this in a firm, measured tone, keeping her keys in her fist, in case she needed to gouge someone's eye out.

Ron came to the door. Reflexively she raised her fist.

"Whoa Madge, what's the matter?" She looked at him and blinked.

"Where is my husband?" She strained to see past his shoulder and shouted. "Bob!"

"Come in, come inside, everything is alright." Ron mumbled. "We're all just talking for Christ sakes."

"I'm not coming in until I see my husband. Bob!"

Just then Frances cried from upstairs, and Madge pushed past Ron and bolted into the living room. Helen and Jimmy were sitting on the couch. Bob was standing there, about to cross the room, when he froze and looked at her. The man she married, had known half her life, was giving her a look she could not decipher, and she felt sick inside, her stomach hollowed, turning into a black pit, drawing her in.

Helen looked at her with a false perplexity. "Madge, you're white as a ghost. Can I get you something, some tea?"

Don't offer me anything in my own house, you fucking bitch. Madge just blinked at her and walked past Ron to go upstairs.

The girls were playing with dolls in the middle of the floor. She calmed herself upon entering the room, slowed her desire to scoop them up and rush them to the car, and asked "Is everything okay, Frances?"

Frances pouted, chin to chest, and held out her doll. The hand was missing. Madge exhaled and sat, cross-legged, on the floor.

"Oh honey, we can fix that. We can fix that easy." She brushed the hair out of her daughter's eyes, looking to Natalie, who calmly pushed her doll's face down into the thick carpet.

"What is everyone doing down stairs?" Natalie held her doll down firmly.

"Talking." Madge sat back, deeply perturbed, and tried to analyze the situation. She thought for a moment. Ron was wearing the same red flannel shirt he had on last week and had smelled a bit rank at the door. She thought she could smell him now and turned. Ron hovered beyond the door frame. He seemed to be moving while standing still, shifting in the shadows of the hallway. She rose and stood between him and the girls.

"Ron, go downstairs." Her voice did not waver.

Again, she considered the keys in her hand a weapon. She gave them a slight bounce in her hand, to feel their heft and hear the familiar jingle. She felt sure she could do it: take out his eyes. She remembered his ax. He stood with open, beckoning hands. She tried to look him in the eyes, to stare him down, but the glare from the ceiling light in the girls' room washed out his glasses into a whitish reflection. He turned and walked back toward the stairway. The doorbell rang. She could hear the front door open, Helen's voice greeting more neighbors, the shuffling off of coats.

She took a step forward when Frances let out a quick, shallow cough. Madge turned and knelt again, pressing her palm on the girl's forehead, feeling Natalie's as well, for good measure. She wasn't sure, but if Frances did not feel a little hot. She dropped her keys and purse and went to her own room to retrieve a thermometer from the medicine cabinet.

CRIVER RAT

River Rat ran wild, claws out, wiry tail whipping the air. Her black calculating eyes searched the block for the inviting hang of any available fire escape. Behind her loomed the Apparition with his dark mouth ringed by shadow. If his darkness reached her, lured her to sleep, she'd be doomed.

A rust-encrusted fire escape hovered above the sidewalk across the street. It gripped a noble pre-war building of crumbling cornices and ornate windowsills sprinkled with spider-plants and plaster Madonnas.

River Rat leapt. The rush of night air slicked her mullet, combing her long whiskers back against her cheeks. Elated, with animal ease she grasped the nearest iron bar and with a minimal twist of her wrist launched her now arrow-straight form up to the second floor landing. Infuriated, the Apparition gathered his grey cloak. The yellow cascade of street lamps blocked his pursuit. He frantically spun about searching for some length of darkness to adhere to, but the building was well lit. Seething, he withdrew as River Rat landed safely on the roof. Proud, shoulders back, her heart racing, the black fur coursing over her tiny breasts shone with sweat. Instinct pulled her out of danger, but the Apparition was a treacherous foe, the scourge of the Lower East Side. This was her second encounter with the villain, her second timely escape. But it would take more than speed to defeat a living shadow.

Villain. The word resonated in River Rat's mind as she leapt from rooftop to rooftop, the Manhattan Bridge drawing near. *I'd never have thought I'd be the one fighting for... something other than myself.* She nearly burst out in laughter, landing softly on dirty tar. Scraps of newspaper churned around a nest of empty beer bottles beside a collapsed chimney. River Rat paused. *It wasn't too long ago I was shoplifting at bodegas. When a young guy walked by me and I was hungry, all I could think about was mugging him.* She shivered and crossed the roof. On the street below, steam snaked out from around the seams of a manhole cover. *I wasn't bad, I was just hungry.* And then she remembered the crimes she had committed when every hunger had been sated.

The Apparition was hungry, too. Only he fed on the souls of the unsuspecting young. So far he had drained the bodies of a college student, a tired mother pushing a stroller heavy with colicky twins, and a drunken tourist who stumbled out of a bar on Ludlow Street; the husks of their corpses discovered in the morning, lines of clear dew streaking their foreheads, beading off lifeless eyes.

She surveyed the street below. Fellow rats pooled at a container of discarded Chinese food. A familial pang rumbled throughout her lithe, furry body. She wanted to join them, to feed. Her tail unconsciously slid up and down her calf in sensual agreement. But for now she was far too restless to dine on whatever delectable trash she could scour from behind a bevy of favorite Clinton Street restaurants. Adrenaline still coursed through her veins and her body wanted to race as fast as her mind. She scurried down the side of a building and crouched between two battered trashcans. Claws draped on silken knees, a whisker twitched. Sniffing at the shadows she almost yearned for the Apparition to return and the chase to resume. *Almost.* When she ran she was free, free from the thoughts of her past that plagued her. River Rat shook herself and stood. It was time for her predawn swim in the East River.

⚭

Before River Rat was River Rat, when she was an ordinary girl (well, there was nothing *ordinary* about her, sleeping on roofs or in parks, begging for change, huffing paint thinner) she knew little of rats, though likely many of the people who rebuffed her while she panhandled in Tompkins Square Park thought of her as nothing more than an out-sized rodent. Still, she no idea if rats were excellent swimmers. No, but her suicide took care of that. Maybe dying was just that; a wealth of information floods you in an instant and a final exasperation supersedes all, as no one ever gets to share this bright, extinguishing knowledge. Except maybe River Rat. Her dive off the Brooklyn Bridge was supposed to be such a Last Act, a final, weary resolution. She desperately wanted to erase her life, the horrible addiction, the scars and scabies, the disgusting acts she had permitted against her body just to have a warm place to stay, the gnawing guilt of having robbed the older, weaker homeless of their change so she could have a midnight meal at McDonalds.

After she stepped off the railing, car horns from the rapidly ascending bridge sounded automotive clarions. A brassy, insane and heavenly jazz called her back up. Scratching at the air, twisting her body away from the rushing massive slab of water, she screamingly wanted to live. Straining desperately against impending death, riled by a shocking, sobering amount of regret and stabbing fear, she reached up toward the bridge and hit the water and died.

And was reborn.

Acutely reborn. Instantly alive to the smell of sewage: not repulsive but *tasty.* Alive to the feel of cold water darkened against a shine of fur. Animal eyes spied a Manhattan transformed, no longer an unlucky prison but a wild sanctuary. She sped toward the nearest seawall. Hungry. Alive, surprised and transformed so completely as to momentarily forget her own name, giving rise to a new determination, the first of many. *I am…new. And new ways must follow. I will allow my old name to fall away when I climb out of this river.*

Ashore, she tested herself. She could see in the dark. And she could move. Quietly, at unimaginable speeds, she could *move*. With a nimble tail that could lift a cinderblock. Sharp nails that could rend a door like paper. She knew she was formidable. *Powerful.* She knew she had returned more than transformed. Where once she had taken, wronged, trespassed and stolen, now she was back to serve. And always, she would remember where she came from.

From now on I am River Rat.

River Rat rested. She had found the most comfortable and appropriate of abodes. Her lair, her perfect nest, was high within the last and largest of the massive, land-bound granite supports of the Manhattan Bridge; an abandoned work room, its ladder of iron bars long rusted away by decades of unrelenting sea air. Larger than some of the studio apartments she'd been in, its tiny wooden door and equally miraculously-unbroken window made a home, a rat-aerie. She retrieved discarded mattresses and stole sheets left out to dry. As dawn broke she would skip across the dented tops of the school buses parked below to launch herself safely homeward. Home. She finally had a home in the city. But some mornings she would pause and look back at the sweeping shadow of the bridge, trying to discern if it hid the waiting form of the Apparition.

She licked her claws clean with a hearty belch that produced an embarrassing flutter of pigeon feathers. As she settled into her nest, the familiar, repetitive thoughts arose. *Did I hit some weird chemical spill in the water? Some nasty nuclear waste? Or maybe I'm like Owlhead, a mutant. Maybe the impact awoke my mutant powers.* She constantly mulled over her transformation. *Mutant.* Was she like the noble Owlhead, indomitably wise, roosting in the top floor of the Chrysler Building, dispensing advice to the authorities while donating vast sums to local charities, coming down to lead the World Guardians against their prospective foes with his vast intellect and frightening telepathic powers? He was a mutant. A rather rotund, preppy mutant—what other crime fighter sported a vest with pocket watch, preferred corduroy to capes, with an obvious penchant for houndstooth? His overly-large human body was capped by a squat befeathered face punctuated by great, lonely eyes above a small, sharp beak that perpetually clasped a smoldering pipe.

River Rat stifled another burp and thought Owlhead would probably frown on her diet of pigeon. There was also the majestic, white-haired Mechanika, a self-made hero, an inventor of extraordinary versatility. Encased in a silver exoskeleton that afforded her great strength and the power of flight (while accentuating a rather amazing ass, River Rat had always blushingly thought) Mechanika was an ally (and rumored ex-lover) to Owlhead, both founding members of the World Guardians.

While still human, River Rat had hung out with friends at Battery Park; cranes rose above the distant construction of the World Guardians' new headquarters, designed by Mechanika, of course, on Governors Island. The group ducked beneath an astonishingly close sonic boom and then scanned the sky. A neon arc of light unfolded across the horizon, ending with the Canadian hero, Light Stream. A shimmering force of human radiance, he hovered over Governors Island, and then disappeared amidst the glass spires. The then-human River Rat was filled with longing, not for the hero, never for anything *male*, but something like flight, something opposite the mordant inadequacy that defined her life, which could only fleetingly be doused by alcohol and drugs.

Those first days after emerging from the frigid, polluted waters, River Rat explored her new agility and powers with a combination of giddiness and determination; she was always smart, no matter how many different drugs clouded her brain. She was always one step ahead of whatever delinquent company she kept. A new purpose rose within her as she stepped from the river. The river did not gift her a tail with which to light a crack pipe. But though she knew of heroes, and in testing her own abilities was confident she at least approached their ranks, River Rat rightly wanted to keep close to the street. The debts she needed to repay were not in the sky, not on Governors Island, but in the gutter.

And so she took to her task with superhuman stealth. If a drunken reveler dropped his wallet she snuck up behind him and dexterously slipped it back into his pocket with her tail. When a couple of young women were accosted by a group of thuggish boys, River Rat sprang from a tree and barred a sharp array of glistening teeth. Two cabbies were close to an altercation when she emerged from the shadows; by simply showing herself, they retreated to their prospective cars, all interest in arguing evaporated (A svelte, 5'4 rodent with daring, dark liquid eyes apparently was an arresting sight).

Recently, the exploits of the Guardians and the war in Iraq, were both pushed off the cover of the Post. Young people were being found dead in the streets of the Lower East Side. Was it a new form of deadly drug overdose? The papers conjectured and wrestled one another for the most shocking photo or graphic coroner quote. Police presence increased. Kids quickened their pace to the subway. The headlines kept coming and the autopsy results were inconclusive, but River Rat smelled murder. She had heard a distant, horrid laughter any night a life was taken. And she knew these lives were being *taken*.

And it was her job to put a stop to it.

After two weeks of prowling and snooping, she saw finally him. *It*. The caped blackness of the Apparition. A cold, rank skeleton wrapped in a foul sheet, hooded, a sick, panting dry mouth permanently open, ready to suck young souls. River Rat readied herself to pounce then paused, thinking it better to observe this creature, size the thing up. It was good that she did. Soon a taxi turned down the street, its headlight beams cast wide. The Apparition withdrew into the shadow of a mailbox, momentarily disappearing. After the taxi passed, the Apparition reappeared across the street, nearly invisible within the darkness directly opposite his original roost. *Ah, so that's his river,* she thought. *He can traverse shadows. So that's how he sneaks up on his victims.* She pulled back from the ledge of the roof.

Well, now I know his power, but when we meet, he won't know mine. River Rat smiled and closed her eyes in concentration. *And no matter how dark it gets at night I'll always know where he is. I know the scent now, that dead, dry rose of death, and he reeks of it.*

When not stalking the very embodiment of death or mangling muggers, River Rat dined. Nocturnal, she slept most of the day. The hypnotic drone of the constant traffic overhead reverberated throughout her rocky womb with a comfortable consistency. She always awoke famished. For starters, fresh pigeon would do (either the little beasts were too stupid or too numerous to realize the ledge in front of her little apartment in the sky might not make for the most benign of layovers). But that was only the first course; the back alleys of Chinatown were a buffet of rotten vegetables and chewed-but-still-lustrous morsels of pork enameled with sweet-and-sour sauce. The pounds of pasta cooling in loosely tied garbage bags behind the Italian eateries on Clinton were nothing short of divine. The best though, was dessert.

The small backyard of the Periwinkle Bakery was a literal oasis, the screen door to the kitchen permanently propped open, inviting the chance cool breeze, all the while releasing the palpably warm scents of fresh baking. Tidy trashcans lined up beside a small garden of herbs and flowers. The leafy fireworks of ornamental cabbage twirled beneath a high fence of mismatched boards crossed with wires heavy from recently rinsed aprons and tablecloths. From the rooftop of a two-story building backing up to the bakery, River Rat secreted herself nightly. After the bakery closed, the cutest girl in an adorably puffy chef's hat aslant across a mop of sweat-soaked hair would step outside and tend to the garden. Wide hips happily stretched checkered pants. Her worn V-neck T-shirt revealed the flour-streaked cleavage of tumbling breasts. The zaftig baker watered plants after placing numerous baking sheets bountiful with left-over cupcakes. She would set them atop the trashcans as neighborhood cats poured through the cracks of the fence to feast.

Whenever the chef re-entered the kitchen to fetch a saucer of milk, River Rat hung off the edge of the building, extended her rear and lassoed a cupcake with her tail. Of course this would startle and confuse the cats. They would scatter while the baker returned with more cupcakes and milk, surprised that the patio had emptied in her brief absence. The baker would squat and whisper velvety nothingness to entice the cats to return. *Here kitty-kitty-kitty.* They would warily poke their heads through the fence while River Rat licked her claws clean, closed her eyes and pretended the sugared whispers were for her pointed, fury ears alone.

Loud construction on the bridge woke her early. Rather than simmer in her hovel, River Rat decided to go for a swim. Parting brown waters, she swam beyond her usual lane beneath the Manhattan Bridge; to give herself a good workout, she headed past the Brooklyn Bridge. In the past she had pushed past logs, always fearful the dark, listless forms would turn out to be a dead body. She had dove and resurfaced to shock sporty pontoon paddlers, and had grown to expect any-and-everything from the filthy river that renewed her life, anything, that is, accept butting heads. In an all-out breaststroke, head down, River Rat experienced a sharp blow. Stunned, she floated slightly backward from the impact, shook herself back to awareness, then brought her knees forward and stretched her arms out to steady herself. Dog-paddling, she faced her grinning obstruction: a green head with a big, friendly smile. Knocked dumb, she returned the smile out of habit, thinking it had been awhile since she had been this close to another person and made eye-contact, much less smiled.

"Hey, I know you."

Another surprise. River Rat realized she hadn't spoken to anyone in months. She opened her mouth and got a mouthful of disgusting water for her efforts. She coughed and sputtered.

"You're River Rat."

A boy bobbed in the water. A large piece of seaweed slipped from his shoulder. Continuing to smile, not bothering to introduce himself, Merboy patiently waited for her coughing to subside. Everyone in the world, everyone that owned a television or had seen a newspaper, knew Merboy. Pulled from a Filipino fisherman's nets and unofficially adopted by the World Guardians as a half-hero, half-mascot. An immediate poster boy for conservation and environmentalism, he had also recently been chastised by the Mayor for skinny-dipping in the Central Park reservoir.

River Rat regained a measure of self-control. "But how did you know my name?'

"Silly, our leader's a telepath. Try cheating on a test when he's even on the same planet." He exaggeratedly rolled his eyes. River Rat instantly warmed to the boy and paddled closer.

"So you all know about me?"

"Of course! Mechanika wants to invite you for dinner, but nobody knows how to cook pigeon."

He giggled, but the water instantly seemed colder. River Rat thought of pushing off into a strong back stoke, but was stilled by the sudden sincerity of the boy's expression.

"Hey. I was joking. It's no problem."

Gracefully, he propelled himself closer with a gentle swipe of webbed fingers. Lowering his voice, "What, you don't think I take a bite out of a catfish now and again out here? I love sushi."

They both laughed. A wave from a distant barge lifted them. River Rat frowned.

"Hey, if you guys know about *me,* then you know I'm dealing with this…this monster on the Lower East Side." Anger rose in her voice. "And I could be killed! And others already have. Maybe I could use a little assistance!"

River Rat glowered and looked down while Merboy considered her comments. She was shocked by her outburst; she hadn't really thought of ever needing help before now.

Merboy spoke calmly: "Hey. Did you see the news last summer, when I led those lost dolphins back out to sea? Could you have done that? Do *you* speak dolphin?"

She opened her mouth to reply, but Merboy continued.

"No, you don't. And neither does Mechanika, and get this: she's a terrible swimmer."

River Rat was perplexed.

"No. Only I could do that. Just like Light Stream was the only one who could fly halfway around the world, and he's the only one who can pass through walls and junk. He entered the cabin of that Air India flight where everyone passed out last month. The pilot and co-pilot were unconscious. He landed that plane safely. I *couldn't* do that."

Merboy looked at River Rat thoughtfully, as if he were speaking to himself just as much as he was talking to her.

"So maybe what's going on in your neighborhood is something you're best suited to take care of."

A whisker twitched in reflexive agreement. She sniffed the air and knew she could follow a thousand different scents to their origin without a problem. She drew closer.

"You know, I'm glad we met."

The membranous mass of a disintegrating trash bag floated past them.

"Yeah." Merboy looked about happily and blinked. River Rat perceived a second pair of transparent eyelids protectively gripping his clear, hopeful eyes.

"Let's hang out again." He leaned in close, startling River Rat by unknowingly mimicking the move of countless boys and older men and too few precious girls who had similarly sought a kiss in the past. She sensed his innocence and kept herself from recoiling.

Merboy whispered. "Don't tell *anyone*, but we're digging an underwater entrance for our new headquarters. Next time, I'll show it to you. That way, you can come over anytime you please. We can play backgammon!" And with that he did a quick somersault, flashing a bare, emerald rump, and then his skinny green legs broke the surface. Long, webbed toes wavered in the air. Waving good-bye with one foot he dove quickly and was gone.

River Rat was surprised and amused. *That little devil was skinny dipping!* She rolled onto her back and launched into a leisurely backstroke.

A congress of cats crowded the loose bricks of the Periwinkle patio. Shoulder to shoulder, they bristled impatiently as the baker laid out baking sheets of fresh cupcakes. She brought an extra mixing bowl of water to supplement the already-drained dish of milk.

River Rat relaxed in respite on the roof above. She scratched a perky ear with her tail and watched her beautiful baker's every move.

More than a dozen pink tongues lapped at mounds of icing. The garden was a quiet frenzy as feasting felines buried their frosted noses further into their individual desserts.

Flour-coated hands on ample hips, the baker squinted and surveyed the skyline.

"I know you're there. Why don't you come down? Don't be afraid. Have a beer with me."

The fur on the back of River Rat's neck stiffened.

The baker squatted on an overturned mop bucket and scanned the rooftops, resolute.

"My name's Maria and I know you're there."

River Rat was shocked that her presence was known, and that for the second time in one day someone was addressing her directly. But this time it was someone she had imagined herself speaking to in her rat-aerie, returning the baker's sweet whispers with animal kisses and little bites and licks. River Rat backed up slowly, more fearful than if the Apparition had called out her discarded human name.

"I *know* you're there. Please. There aren't enough cats in all of New York City to eat the number of cupcakes I've been laying out lately."

River Rat paused and sucked at the crumbs between her sharp teeth.

"So c'mon, show yourself. I won't judge you –I just want to see who I'm feeding."

She had forded the East River moments after what should have been her demise, danced across rooftops with the Grim Reaper's gross cousin. Yet now, River Rat pulled back quickly and quietly, launching herself across the street, noisily latching onto a fire escape to evade…what? Why was she running?

Back in her lair, River Rat crawled along the walls. *Not exactly a love nest, is it? I mean, I can't really bring her back here, can I? There aren't even any stairs, no ladder!*

She attacked her mattress until distended springs stirred a flurry of shredded fabric. Settling into one corner, ankles crossed, head in her arms, she cried. She cried the East River, a cold current that forever flushed the debris of eight million souls out into a forgiving sea, an ocean so huge that it could blithely absorb all toxins, maternally washing away the salt of a city's sorrow. River Rat dried her eyes. She had swam a river in the morning and made a friend, treated the entire Lower East Side as if it were her private trough and ended up marveling at a fine girl who dared to notice her presence and tell River Rat her name.

It was time for one more swim.

River Rat rose, kicked open the door and dove into the shadows.

The Apparition supped deeply. He dropped the nearly lifeless boy beside a swing set in a small brick park attached to a group of closely-knit housing projects. The monster ran an obsidian tongue across the cursive tattoo alighting the boy's once-bronze neck, now pale and dry, an empty reed pending his soul's complete removal. The boy was nearly a child, daring the night in a sleeveless jean jacket, copious bands accenting multi-veined wrists. Knuckles sagged as his hands unclenched in ultimate surrender.

The Apparition readied his hideous laugh as a brick struck the back of his head. Involuntarily, he coughed out the boy's soul. The youth was gripped by seizure. They coughed in unison as bits of brick spackled the miniature playground. Light returned to rightful owner, the kid was on his knees while the soul-stealer scanned the block for his attacker. Dazed, the boy didn't know what happened, but he knew he had had more than the breath knocked out of him, and that it was time to get home *fast*.

The Apparition slowly looked up. River Rat waved "hello" from atop the Holiday Inn, blocks away, across Roosevelt Park. The thing convulsed in anger, knowing she stood at too great a distance to even consider a pursuit. By now the boy had sprinted to the nearest subway entrance and had vanished underground. A cold scream replaced the Apparition's typically cruel cackle. The vermin of Roosevelt Park scurried away, but River Rat stood resolute, the moon at her shoulder shone like a steady, permanent shield.

Famished, River Rat rode the rooftops toward the bakery. It was late and likely the cats had consumed all of the cupcakes while her cute pastry-chef had turned out the lights and gone home. The sharp scent of discarded sushi about to turn caught her attention. River Rat vaulted over a satellite dish to dumpster dive behind a Japanese restaurant.

Several blocks away, Maria sat on an overturned milk crate surrounded by guttering candles, a half-drunk bottle of Cabernet between her feet, a wasted picnic of gnawed sandwiches and cookie crumbs strewn about. She wept against balled-up fists.

With every tear, a cupcake would burst like popcorn on the laundry line. Another tear and a giant, vibrantly fluffy pastry would materialize at the end of an overhanging branch.

She knuckled away a bubble of snot. With a quick sneeze, a rainbow shower of sprinkles began to fall from the sky. A few sugary morsels bounced off her forehead as she looked up. Exasperated, she raced back into the kitchen to fetch a mixing bowl with which to catch the bounty.

The soft ping of sprinkles rolling around the metallic basins resounded like a lonely pachinko parlor as she settled into the kitchen doorway. Cats returned in droves to eat the cupcakes out of the trees, swiping vainly at the bulky ones hanging off the laundry line, purring in anticipation. She took a swig of wine straight from the bottle. This happened whenever she was sad. Cupcakes appeared. A summer shower of sprinkles sugared the room. However, when it was actually time to bake, no amount of concentration could produce the slightest pastry. Both her passion and vocation, Maria baked all day. But a certain song on the radio played and cupcakes would appear on the windowsill like confectionary mushrooms. A melodramatic midnight movie on TV and she would have a lap filled with pastry by the time the credits rolled. Curse or talent, she struggled to hide this ability from everyone she knew. Her last almost-girlfriend had broken up with her in a restaurant, holding her hand in that annoying grip of sympathy and comfort, saying "Lovely Maria, you're just too sweet."

Maria had rolled her eyes. Her date exaggeratedly nodded in compassion, thinking Maria was shocked and disappointed when really Maria thought *you really have no idea.*

The sprinkle-shower ceased. She plucked a large cupcake from the laundry line and ruefully took a bite. Frosting stuck to the back of her throat. A mouthful of sugary frosting and all she could taste were her own tears.

As the sun set River Rat, plunged into murky waters, her eyes stinging from the diesel-laced effluvia that coated the river. She hoped to catch some fish for dinner and was out longer than usual, eager for another chance meeting with Merboy. She held her breath underwater and watched the fresh white wake of the Circle Line dissipate, having weighed the fun in surfacing close to the boat to give the tourists something to gape at, versus the multiple camera flashes that would surely send her photo to the front page of the Post. She coolly chose to hover below, her mission best served if she remained urban legend rather than media sideshow.

Breaking the surface, she looked for the Manhattan Bridge to get her bearings. Seagulls complained overheard. By now it was obvious Merboy wouldn't be putting in an appearance. Launching into a backstroke, River Rat kicked toward shore. She hoped to see her new green friend again soon, and resolved to make an effort of it—possibly she would swim over to Governors Island. But before that, she needed to emerge from the shadows and introduce herself to the nice young girl who had been making her more than just dessert these past few weeks.

"Hi."

A spatula dropped, impressing an areola of whipped-cream on to the thick rubber mat. Maria turned toward the dark cameo behind the screen door. Quickly composing herself, she licked her teeth and tried for a casual smile.

"There you are." Voluptuous fingers swiped the chef's hat off her sweaty brow and fluffed her thick, spiky crimson locks to life. The silhouette behind the door nodded, less an acknowledgement and more out of personal satisfaction…River Rat had always liked redheads. She then rushed toward the shadows as Maria swung the screen door open.

"Wait! I have some cheese sandwiches and a Coke for you."

River Rat smiled at the song of her voice and stifled a giggle at the thought that she should, after all, *really* like cheese.

From the shadows: "I'm…I'm *different*."

Maria's smile pushed up against full, flush cheeks. "Aren't we all? Look, if you're sleeping rough, its okay with me, I just want us to get to know each other. I mean, I know you've been coming around for awhile now, and I guess you like my cupcakes."

She blushed. River Rat stirred.

"So show yourself." Maria turned back toward the kitchen and reached for a plate of sandwiches.

"Let me see you. Please." She held the plate out, a peace offering, a meal made just for River Rat. The first in a very long time.

River Rat slowly unwound her long tail out of the darkness and let it sway playfully in the moonlight. Maria gasped and dropped the dish. River Rat instinctively lunged and caught the airborne sandwiches in one claw, the plate in another. Back leg extended, body bent as if she were taking a bow, she looked up at Maria and smiled. River Rat realized she was probably showing more sharp teeth than she should when meeting someone for the first time. She studied Maria's gaze intently. Maria returned an equally penetrating look.

She was not afraid.

Maria cocked her head and examined River Rat, who slowly rose. A whisker twitched (that cheese certainly *did* smell enticing). They scrutinized one another. River Rat wanted to lean in and lick the little ear peeking out from her thick, luscious hair. Embarrassed by the thought, she took a step back, found the upended milk crate and sat with her sandwiches. Stunned, Maria took a step backwards as well. Without taking her eyes off River Rat she fumbled with the screen door, pulled it open and reached for a Coke. She drank half of it before handing it to River Rat. As their fingers met Maria almost jumped; the fur of sharp fingers brushing against her flesh produced an electrical charge.

The Apparition stalked the shuttered storefronts along Delancey Street. Appalled by the well-lit rise of the Williamsburg Bridge, he slinked down a darker street and gathered the shredded ends of his cape about him. Stationary, he hoped to make a meal of a passing club kid or Chinese delivery boy. Hunger emboldened him. Angry thoughts bubbled in the tar pit of his black brain. *That rat girl thwarted my feeding for the last time.* A new, sharper appetite flicked open like a switch blade within the creature: revenge. And revenge carved new thoughts. *Where does that rat girl live?* The Apparition had floated through the city for decades, drifting toward whatever soul happened to be near, the younger the better. He had never truly *hunted*, made conscious decisions, recalled memories or lived for anything more than the night.

Not until now.

His long, sinewy fingers emerged from the protective shadows of the lamppost and gripped its cold iron neck. The appearance of River Rat served as an awakening. He dimly recalled his previous life as a disconnected mass of roaches feeding on muck in a forgotten subway tunnel. A subspecies blind and inbred, indifferent to the soldiers in strange suits and masks who quietly filled the tunnel with a thick gas. They held out rods and took readings and watched with clinical curiosity as the homeless men encamped within clutched at their throats and died. The fumes tortured the insects as well. They furiously swarmed, scattering and reforming in agony, a fruitless attempt to escape the burning poison. Thwarted by the gas, they settled onto the dirty corpse of a young man bent over a cold rail, his body strong and still warm. The harried insects forced their way down his throat, burrowed into his skin, linked like black armor across his chest. The gas settled. Acidic chemicals melted and warped the insects into black oil that slowly seeped into the pores of their chosen host. And the soldiers left and the corpses rotted. And in this warren of death and darkness something fermented.

That something was the Apparition, shocked into the semblance of life by an errant jolt of electricity. He crawled his way to the surface and greeted an indifferent city with a malevolent appetite.

He hung from the lamppost and barred his black lips and gritted obsidian teeth. The memory of his painful transformation, the deep hunger forced upon him by River Rat, served to hone his instincts and awoke a forgotten insect attribute.

The Apparition gathered his cape and smoothed it against his back. It billowed, shot through with pulsing veins. The creature felt his body lengthen as he readied himself.

Let the rodent keep her gutter. I will once again fly.

∽

Maria reveled in finally being able to reveal her secret. They laughed and drew closer as Maria described her numerous misadventures with spontaneously appearing cupcakes. River Rat relaxed. The other girl's desire to share set River Rat at ease. And they did share, though River Rat was unsure how to tell her story, Maria did not press, fascinated as she was by the thick down that covered her skin, the long tail that seemed to be everywhere at once, brushing Maria's ankle, gently cupping the back of her head. Emboldened, River Rat told of her meeting with Merboy. Suitably impressed, Maria spoke of the celebrities addicted to her cupcakes. Both spoke of the difficulties they faced as teenagers, though River Rat withdrew slightly and stopped short of giving specifics; they understood that this would take time. They were just getting to know each other and not everything needed to be revealed at once.

The moon was wistful, graciously parting grey clouds. Several strays dozed at their feet. Maria went into the kitchen to fetch a bottle of wine. She needed the moment alone. Her mind was a feverish blend of surprise, delight, fear and anticipation. She swallowed and looked around for a corkscrew. The wine would lead to their first kiss. She was both worried and excited about the sharpness of River Rat's teeth. And she blushed at the thoughts she was having about the touch of her tail.

In the garden, River Rat licked the palms of her hands and smoothed back her hair. She stretched, content, unconcerned that dawn wasn't too far away. Several of the cats stirred. One hissed. River Rat listened but only heard Maria rattling around inside. She relaxed and closed her eyes to better taste the scents of sugar, sweat and desire drifting from the kitchen.

A sharp shadow cut across the moon unobserved as Maria reappeared with a bottle of wine and two glasses.

The following week was blissful. They met every night after the Periwinkle closed. They dined under the stars and kissed and more. River Rat was surprised at her own assertions. And Maria enjoyed each and every one, relieved to have met someone willing to hold her down but not hold her back; she wanted what she had to give to be taken from her, drawn out with small bites and nips. Conversely, the city seemed well-behaved. River Rat had pulled a drunken NYU student out of traffic, but encountered no crime. She even worried she was too caught up in her newfound relationship, that possibly she was not vigilant enough, and so doubled her efforts to police the Lower East Side.

From one of her favorite perches, on the roof of the Gothic library nestled in the corner of Seward Park, River Rat caught a familiar, sweet scent. Impossible. Her whiskers twitched as she leaned into the wind. She rushed to the back of the building, turned and took a running leap and easily bridged the street below. Landing roughly on the roof of an austere apartment building under renovation, she moved among large, dusty plastic sheets flapping from beneath piles of new brick. A large cupcake sat atop a chimney. The aroma was delicious: curlicues of sugary frosting punctuated with a rainbow of sprinkles atop a moist dessert. She greedily consumed it, licking every crumb from her claws. She tasted the girl she loved. And something more, something floral, alluring.

River Rat hiccupped and thought of the peculiarity of this midnight snack: *how did Maria get up here and why?* It didn't make any sense but before she could puzzle it out the scent of yet another hypnotic dessert caught her attention. She was drawn to it. Jumping, she barely made it to the next roof, but was too transfixed to notice her slightly intoxicated state.

Maria waited patiently for the last two customers to finish. She was eager to close and rendezvous with her lover. *Lover.* She considered the word. *Am I dating a hero or someone like myself, a lost little girl?* The couple rose, grabbed their bags and pushed away from the table. Maria locked up behind them and bused the table. As the dishes sunk into tepid, sudsy water her contemplative mood returned: *or maybe the difference between the two isn't so great now that we've found each other.* But there was a very big distinction. River Rat's abilities translated into something meaningful, Maria felt her unusual gift was… worthless. She sighed and emptied out the register. She stopped counting money and surveyed the room. The walls were decorated with musical instruments and masks, wild faces from festivals and carnivals. They too, seemed frivolous. But she thought of the World Guardians, their costumes, of River Rat's velvet fur. *For some, did a mask, a costume, help channel their abilities?* She pulled a simple black Mardi Gras mask off the wall. Maria blew the dust off and positioned it daintily above her nose. She turned toward the open saloon doors of the kitchen and concentrated upon the skillet resting on the stove. Eyes closed, fists clenched tight, she thought sweet thoughts, imagined massive revolving cupcakes. Maria opened her eyes. The skillet was disappointingly empty. She shrugged and entered the kitchen. Pulling off her apron, she sighed and stepped out onto the back porch, hoping River Rat would be there to offer a distraction from her latest failure. While outside, she failed to hear the light rain of sprinkles filling the frying pan.

River Rat reeled, dizzy and confused. Pulled forward by yet another well-placed cupcake, she devoured it but felt both nauseous and ravenous. The underlying scent was familiar yet distant. Every time she blinked she wanted to keep her eyes closed. She stumbled to the ledge and fell over. Landing hard on the roof of the next building below, the breath knocked out of her, River Rat tried to rise. The black tar was decorated with a large swirl of cupcakes. Each one was more beautiful than the next. The largest central cupcake promised a sweetness that made her mouth water. She swooned and fell forward, crushing the closest cupcake. A particular scent wafted up. Her whiskers twitched. The dead, dry rose of death spiced the air. *This is a trap. A trap laid by the Apparition.* Desperately, she tried to regain her senses. Standing, vertigo struck. River Rat fell into the arms of a shadow. And the shadow comforted her. She felt peace. As darkness cradled her, her breathing became shallow. She began to dream.

River Rat dreamed she was back on the Brooklyn Bridge.

As the screen door swung shut behind her, Maria saw a liquid shadow race across the gutter. She gritted her teeth and felt an instant suspicion. River Rat had described her nemesis well. The night was freakishly still. Maria cocked her head. She heard a weak exhalation and then nothing. She raced toward the fire escape.

River Rat was perched on one of the steel girders of the Brooklyn Bridge. It was nighttime and traffic rushed by below. Her fur bristled in the wind but she did not feel cold. Or scared. This time when she jumped she would not fall. She would fly into the wind and tumble into nothingness, roll into a cloud and dissipate. And yet she lingered, one claw wrapped around a cold cable. The ocean below reflected a deep oblivion. She looked up and searched the sky for the moon and was troubled by the starless, black canvas above. The darkness tugged, her grip on the cable loosened.

"River Rat!"

A shout awakened her. But all was still obscured by darkness. The Apparition's deadly maw loomed close, breathing in her soul. Her head hung limp as the creature held her by her wrists. She slowly opened her eyes as Maria came over edge of the roof. Fear awoke her further as she tried to call out and warn Maria away. But the darkness was too powerful. She was drawn toward the black whirlpool of his mouth. Again, she smelled roses. And there she saw a speck of light. A tiny morsel of whiteness rotated and rapidly grew. Soon a cupcake clogged the Apparition's mouth. He let go of River Rat and brought his hands to his throat as the cake expanded and stretched his jaws. The creature furiously twisted and turned and still the cupcake grew.

Crumbs dropped onto River Rat as she shook herself back to full consciousness.

Maria strode across the roof confidently. She never took her eyes off the Apparition as River Rat crawled toward her. And with a sick snap, the Apparition's lower jaw broke. A vile liquid poured out as the creature collapsed. Maria rushed to River Rat's side as the thing convulsed and further dissembled. The Apparition was now a pool of oil bubbling around a giant cupcake stained black. Strange insect shapes simmered to the surface and dissolved.

Maria held River Rat's head in her lap. A feverish sweat moistened her brow as she took in the darkly radiant skyline. She held out her hand and concentrated. A small cupcake appeared in her palm. Gingerly, she took a bite. It no longer tasted of tears.

The Next Bardo

Bardo, Noun. In Tibetan Buddhism, the state between death and rebirth which varies… depending on the person's conduct in the previous life and their age at and manner of death.

Dictionary.com

As a travel writer, I might not make much money but I've certainly seen a lot, and know how to track down a lead. So it was with an immeasurable amount of surprise, while editing an upcoming anthology, *Best Gay Bars Ever*, that one of the submissions concerned an establishment in my hometown of Avondale, Florida. I've always said that being gay makes you a natural detective, or it used to be before you could watch cute boys make out in the back of a bus on MTV (I worry that what ever little extra bit of extrasensory perception we've got will be lost as we become more acceptable, more "mainstream"). I had taken on the task of compiling this book by following the one rule that's kept me employed all these years: never say "No." If a publisher asks, no matter what they ask, I say "Yes," deliver on-time, and hope that the next job is one in-line with my interests and skills (which is how I once wrote an unenviable 5,000 words, "Gay Nightlife in Buffalo," by poetically describing nearly every song on the jukebox of the one gay bar in town).

Best Gay Bars Ever (the publisher's title, not mine) was supposed to be a quickie, not much writing, more a compendium of people talking up their favorite joints; all I had to do was verify their existence, note their address and hours and organize it by state and city, letting the patrons do the rest. Well the call got all sorts of snide e-mails and over-the-top glowing reviews obviously from the hands of owners and managers, along with some smart and witty observations from genuinely supportive clientele. I culled additional entries from old guidebooks and friend's suggestions. What I had not expected were the memories. Well-typed (from real type writers, on bonded paper, no less!) or hand-written letters telling me about gay bars in the fifties and sixties, one from the forties, some with barely perceptible lines of scrawl detailing everything about these now long-gone bars; safe havens, oasis' of honesty in dark times when men who loved men were deemed sick degenerates brutalized by the police, and assassinated by the press. Some of this writing read like good-bye letters, the writers long retired, often from tony addresses in New York City or Palm Springs and also, surprising places like Minnesota and even Alaska. Though there was no place for these reminisces in the anthology several of them were quite moving. All of them were of historical interest. I toyed with the idea of pulling together another anthology or at least saluting these faded taverns in some sort of post script, maybe even seeing if any of the authors of these letters had photographs or memorabilia to include.

None of this deterred me from my deadline; the publisher, though small, considered this a priority project with a large run (for a gay audience anyway), meaning there might be some real money in it for me. Still, a letter about a bar in my hometown that *I* didn't know about was a bit of a revelation. It simply stated that The Next Bardo was a piano bar above a bookshop on Main Street in Avondale,

Florida -operated from the mid-seventies to the late eighties, closing upon the passing of the owner.

Well, if it opened in the seventies, that would explain the cheesy name, but no that's impossible, I finished high school in 1980. I shopped at that very bookstore on Main Street. I remembered holding the worn paperback copy of Patricia Neil Warren's The Frontrunner *in my trembling hands. I was still in high school when I found that book; I was so electrified by the cover; two men close together and the blurb "an unusual love story" seared my brain. Never mind that the word "unusual" would now be heartily panned; it was the pairing of "love" and "story" that shook my world. Up until then everything I'd secretly read about homosexuality had been in psychology books coldly debating whether it was an affliction or a natural occurrence. I had yet to see "gay" linked with "love." I was enthralled but still too scared to buy the book in my home town, at a store where I could easily be recognized. I quickly memorized the cover, the author's name, and left to drive one hour to the mall in another town to buy the book. Even then I was so scared about what possessing the book meant about who I was that I kept it in the trunk of my car, lest my parents find it in my room and think I was a sick pervert. I rushed through the book and loved every page. But still, in the middle of the night, I woke up gripped by intense paranoia. If I were ever killed in a car accident the book would be found in the trunk of my car. I slipped out of the house and retrieved it; the next morning I grimly deposited it in a mailbox on the way to school and didn't read another gay book until after college.*

That memory had always shamed me; that I had been so close to liberation but had allowed fear to override everything. Sure, I was only sixteen and that the coming out process takes time. Those feelings seem so ancient, so distant from today's reality; I couldn't help but relate to the letters I had received. Once again I looked at the letter about The Next Bardo: strong cursive. Signed but undated. The return address Tampa; an hour's drive from Avondale. All the more reason to finish the book: the book's release party had already been planned and set for a new gay bookstore near Las Olas Avenue in Fort Lauderdale. Not close to Tampa, by any means, but once I was back in Florida, I'd definitely look the writer of the letter up, and gather more information about The Lost Bardo.

The gay publishing world being what it is, the release party never came to fruition as the book's publication was delayed for the holiday market (the upcoming spring and travel market was deemed "too soft"). So I concentrated on other projects. I wrote about a quick trip to Oaxaca for an airline's in-flight magazine, and would forget about these long gone gay bars until another letter would belatedly appear in my P.O. Box. I would savor the well-written ones, and had even engaged in a flurry of correspondence with an elderly gentleman in Chicago who had brave tales to tell of tail-end prohibition and how the speakeasy culture transferred into an early gay underground. Marvelous stuff. I was considering traveling to Chicago to interview him when I got an offer from a major newspaper to travel to Tarpon Springs and write about it for their "48 Hours In-" series. I jumped at the assignment and booked my flight the same day I accepted the offer. Not only was I itching to get away from rainy, frigid New York, but thoughts of secret bars in Chicago had rekindled my interest in The Lost Bardo. Avondale was an easy drive away.

I rushed through Tarpon Springs, did the touristy things, ate early appetizers at three restaurants close together so I could write as if I had had two lunches and a dinner, then went back to the hotel to call information. The writer of the letter didn't have a listed number. I knew the area and I knew that with interstate traffic I could be at his address by sunset, not too late for a friendly knock at the door. While driving down Highway 19, I rolled the windows down to let the balmy air fill the rental car. Miles of lush green overgrowth and tacky billboards whipped by. *Oh my god, what if he's married? A lot of these older guys were so closeted.* I ever so slightly eased up on the gas and thought that, if I sensed he didn't live alone, I might just claim to be lost, or looking for a neighbor; I wasn't about to shatter an old man's façade simply to satisfy my curiosity.

I turned off the highway and made a few turns, pulling over to consult one of the laminated maps stocked in the glove box. What I remembered of Tampa had been devoured by suburbs and strip malls, but I was familiar with the street the letter writer lived on. Or I should say was buried near. I rolled to a stop as dusk drained the color from the sky. Black birds came to rest on the brick arch of a small, poorly kept cemetery. A groundskeeper with his back to me fixed the padlock and lumbered away. I checked the address on the letter again, and stopped the car and got out.

Skinny, nearly denuded palm trees twisted up out of the ground on either side of the cemetery gates. I peered through the distressed chain link fence. Rows of tombstones listed into piles of palmetto brush. Sprinklers burst to life, flushing out a few more birds which flapped lazily to settle on nearby telephone lines. Even though it was typically humid, I held my arms for warmth. It was as if a negative magnetism emanated from the cemetery, a reverse undertow that pushed me back; I was literally repelled toward my car. Shocked that I felt cold, I stopped myself from turning on the heat. I quickly pulled away and headed down the road -the warm wind on my face.

Back at the hotel I let the banalities of the local news drone on the television as I changed into my swimsuit. I looked at myself in the mirror as the tanned and bleach blonde jockish weatherman bragged about the pending perfect weather. I had been able to loose the weight I had gained after my boyfriend of ten years and I had broken up. My hair was thinning in what I hoped was a distinguished manner. I had a moustache that I considered roguish rather than dated, but now I was unsure. Writing for travel magazines and guidebooks, I had come to expect, and even savor, the unexpected, but I had not anticipated that my day would end at a graveyard. I had driven around the neighborhood until the sun had completely set trying to sort through my confusion and dread. On the freeway I listened to talk radio, something I never did, so I wouldn't feel alone. Now I hurried to the pool, half hopeful that it would be filled with annoying children trying to pull some last bit of fun out of the day before their exhausted and sunburned parents ordered them to bed. The pool was empty. Clumps of soggy towels clotted on the sagging straps of chaise lounge chairs; the blue waters of the pool beckoned. I slipped into the warm and too-chlorinated waters and was rejuvenated, Awoken from my stupor, hungry, I dove and emerged renewed, determined to work on my promised article all night if need be, so I could then focus on the mystery of The Next Bardo.

I resisted returning to the cemetery; I didn't want to waste time searching for a grave that would likely only give me a name I already had. Up early to beat the morning traffic, Avondale was an hour away; during the drive over I thought about my parents and ruminated on whether I should have visited them more before their passing. Our memories of my childhood were so conflicting, so many arguments ended with them saying "You've changed," and I whispering to myself after I'd hung up the phone, "No, this is who I've always been." Now I was returning to my hometown for the first time since their deaths. It felt discourteous and selfish that I always made excuses to not visit when they were alive, to come now on an investigative whim.

I drove straight to the memorial park where their urns were placed in a columbarium. Unnerved, this being my second, unplanned visit to a cemetery, I waited for the florist across the street to open. Craving a cigarette like I hadn't in years, I fought off the urge to call my ex-boyfriend. I'd quit all those years ago due mostly to his pleading and badgering. He should be the one to talk me through moments like this. Our relationship had drifted into one of those friendships of necessity, however. Now and then he called with theater gossip, not because he thought I cared but because the threads of our shared experiences were so intertwined that they formed the basis of our current, separate reality; I was the only one who got his little jokes. If he didn't tell me then it detracted from his understanding; just like when I re-visit somewhere that we had traveled to together. I might write a new piece from an entirely new perspective, but the pivot of that point of view was his arms around me in a variety of hotel rooms around the world.

I had trouble finding their urns; I don't pray, so I tried to think of something that would please them both. A light wind rustled the surrounding palm fronds. A stooped elderly man, his pants high on his waist, quietly hobbled past, a toothbrush in his hand. He bent at an odd angle, loudly mustered a gob of spit and lobbed it at the name plate of a mausoleum, then began scrubbing away with the toothbrush. Smiling, buoyed by his sacrilegious devotion, I went back to the car to drive downtown.

The bookstore was still in business and had just opened. The girl behind the counter was too young to have worked there long enough to give me any useful information so I browsed. I checked the travel section to see if any of my books were in stock. There was nothing of mine. Apparently no gay section either.

A large cat ignored me in the used paperback section. I nostalgically skimmed the titles to see if they had a copy of *The Frontrunner*, but they didn't. I brought the local paper to take with me to a dinner and over breakfast tried to think of who I could look up that might have some information about The Next Bardo.

Memories of high school returned: the only other kid I thought was gay, who everyone thought was gay, was Franklin, a smallish, impossibly pale youth with hair so blonde it shone white in the afternoon sun. Growing up in Florida, everyone was naturally tan and spent an inordinate amount of time outdoors, so he was an easy target for teasing. Worse, there was nothing he could do to vanquish his effeminacy, no way he could butch things up a bit; he was just too lithe and attractive to pass for a typical boy of that or any era. High School in the seventies was all about long hair and getting stoned. Or being a jock. I was able to secret myself within a fog of marijuana and fortify a believable personality behind a truly impressive record collection, but poor Franklin stuck out, not only because he was so pale but because he was so talented. He sang like an angel. We would snicker in the back row at attendance-mandatory choral concerts in the school auditorium.

He was just too different, smart and articulate. In English, the teacher typically only spoke to him when we dissected Shakespeare. Junior year I saw him at a Styx concert. He was alone and I was with a group of stoners. He smiled and I turned my back on him, and in essence, turned my back on myself. Worse, I had a huge crush on the band's guitarist, Tommy Shaw. I stared at his long, streaming blonde hair and felt trapped by embarrassment and desire so I lit another joint.

Shamefully, I tried to remember Franklin's last name and wondered if he still lived in Avondale; maybe he had visited The Next Bardo. I was sure he left town one minute after graduation. We always leave. It's the only way to find ourselves.

I spent the rest of the afternoon at the courthouse researching business licenses and tax information on an antiquated microfiche machine. Though I expected the answer, I still let out a deep breath upon verifying that the man who sent the letter had indeed owned the bar. The records room was overly air-conditioned and I rubbed my hands for warmth; ridiculously I even tested the air to see if my breath was visible. I departed and lingered by my car in the parking lot, letting the Florida sun warm my pale skin. Part of me wanted to head to the beach and forget the whole thing. Maybe it was some demented former patron playing a joke -but the letter folded in my shirt pocket weighed heavier than a mere prank.

After lunch, I went downtown to the library. I spent an hour going through the obituaries from the year the bar had closed; his death notice was small. No next of kin listed. In 1985 death from "cancer" for young or unmarried middle-aged men was code for AIDS.

I strolled back over to the bookstore. Sure enough, the young girl at the counter had been replaced by a much older man. He was obviously one of those wonderfully snobbish small town arbiters of taste, dispensing wisdom for an entire community, coddling old mystery-loving ladies, outliving any number of store cats, naming their replacements with appropriately Dickensian names. His librarian glasses hung from a string of flamboyant beads; I introduced myself and told him I was on assignment but had been born here. Putting on his glasses and tipping his head back, we talked books, how much the town had changed (in my private observation, hardly at all; in his loud lament, everything had been ruined by retiring "Yankees"). He made a few restaurant recommendations which I considered my "in." I asked about The Next Bardo and with a practiced tilt of his head he let his glasses drop from his nose. He looked over my shoulder and back through the years. I worried that I might have hit a nerve but he smiled and whispered, "If you're looking for a drink, I suggest you go to Ladybug's. They should be open now and the happy hour crowd consists of just the old crows you'd be looking for."

The bell above the door jingled and a gaggle of elderly women in loose flowing sun dresses and giant Jackie O. sunglasses entered and rushed the bookseller with a cackle of gossipy rejoinders about books he'd recommended and special orders that had yet to arrive. He grinned and positioned his glasses back onto the bridge of his nose, whispered an address to me and scooped up the feline that had been purring at his feet.

Typical of small town gay bars, Ladybug's was off the beaten path. I walked a few blocks toward the bay and turned down a water laden back alley. A rainbow colored scarab painted onto a picturesque wooden plank hung above a dinted metal door. The door opened onto a narrow stairwell. The walls were dirty and the steps creaked. At the top of the stairs I parted a heavy curtain of painted beads and entered a festive saloon crowded with a tropical motif. Fake banana leaf fans spun lazily from a ceiling festooned with a variety of dusty holiday decorations and balloons. The old men at the bar all turned to look at me. They were probably expecting another of the regulars and quickly turned back toward their drinks or each other;

the bartender, an older tanned man in a Hawaiian shirt and requisite Lai shot me a quick smile. I nodded, surveyed the bar one more time and asked for "something tropical."

"I make a mean Mai Tai," he said with a wink and went to work on the concoction. I nestled up to the bar as the jukebox began to play one of my favorite songs, *Don't Leave Me This Way*, by Thelma Houston. Comfortable, I over-tipped and took a sip of my drink. The soulful, melancholic lyrics of the song, and the strength of the alcohol, were relaxing. One of my fellow patrons fished a pack of cigarettes from out of his shirt pocket and walked toward a sliding glass door, what I had originally thought was just a window obscured by the same beads that covered the door. I let him have a few moments to himself before I grabbed my drink and joined him. The porch was thin but long, opening to an amazing view of the bay. Sailboats rocked back and forth. Brilliant sunlight glinted off the water. I asked the man how long he'd lived in Avondale.

"Five years," he replied. "Retired here from Missouri. Where are you from?" His reply and question were appropriately noncommittal, so I engaged in a little chitchat. When he offered a cigarette I passed, and, excusing myself from temptation, went back inside.

The bar seemed darker, more immersed in shadow. As my eyes adjusted, a Donna Summers song filled the room. In my brief absence a few more regulars had come in and I'd lost my seat at the bar. I went over to the jukebox and flipped through the selections: the expected Cher, the revelation of some serious jazz. I decided that if I was going to pump this room for information I had better prepare to stay awhile so I fed the jukebox a five dollar bill and began selecting songs. My course of music, mostly long versions of disco classics, was approved by all and of course it was the old New Yorker in the bar that started talking first and loudest. The early days of the Paradise garage were praised, the death of Times Square lamented; though he, too, hadn't been in Avondale long enough to be informative, I used my newfound camaraderie with him to chat up the bartender. I ordered another Mai Tai, introduced myself, told him I grew up here and asked if he remembered The Next Bardo. He nodded coolly and asked if I'd frequented it.

"No, I was still in high school at the time. I just knew about it. It was above the bookstore, if I recall."

"Well, I tended bar there until it closed. The owner was the first person I knew who got sick." He poured a variety of liquors into the glass, then reached for the top shelf and retrieved a dark brown bottle without a label. Since he dusted it off with a washcloth, I knew he hadn't used this particular alcohol for my first drink. Filling the rest of my glass, he added a golden wedge of pineapple and said, "But not the last."

I tipped heavily again but before I could ask another question he moved down to the other end of the bar to refill some drinks. I talked a bit more about New York with the guy next to me. I was familiar with his story: early retirement trading culture, intellectual conversation and mass transportation for good weather, meaning he was desperate to convince any one who would listen that he was *happy*. I listened politely. This drink was more potent than the first. The after-work crowd arrived; a younger set that paid attention only to each other, laughing loudly, frequently letting themselves out onto the porch to smoke. One by one, the older patrons said their goodbyes and slipped away.

The former New Yorker invited me to dinner but I declined and repositioned myself at the bar. My big tip aside, the bartender was doing his best to ignore me and pay close attention to the few remaining regulars. The sun had set and someone had left the sliding glass door open so a cool evening breeze drifted in and settled the bar. I finished my drink and stood to go out to the porch to take in the view, but I felt drunk and nauseous. Puzzled—I've always held my liquor—I lurched toward the bathroom, worried I might actually throw up. The room tilted; the lights dimmed as I hurried into one of the stalls and then felt fine. Glad that the moment had passed, I relieved myself and washed up.

While splashing water on my face, I was surprised that the bathroom wasn't adorned with the same tropical decorations as the rest of the bar. The facilities were elegant, the fixtures polished antiques -cloth towels were folded politely within a wicker basket. A black comb levitated in a cylinder of blue liquid. Mildly perplexed, I decided I'd had enough for the night and that it was time to head back to the hotel. Back in the bar, the atmosphere had substantially changed. During my brief time in the bathroom the place had filled with beautiful men, and women, too. Everything was different. Gone were the florid curios and decorations. Instead, a layer of smoke clung to the ceiling. *People were smoking indoors, how decadent!* I turned to ask the bartender what was going on and was shocked to see that he was wearing a tuxedo. He was much younger than I recalled but he gave me a courteous nod and presented me a freshly poured drink.

"Compliments of the owner." With that he turned his back and begun making a martini. I was utterly confused, as if I had just gotten off an airplane in the wrong country. So I grabbed my drink and walked around the room: the patrons seemed as if they were of a dream, too. Dressed from different eras, men in suits stood beside boys with feathered hair and unbuttoned Genera shirts; two women in matching men's clothing and long strands of pearls shared a cigarette dangling from a long cigarette holder. I took a swig of my drink, then another and closed my eyes, trying to identify it by its unsettlingly familiar yet elusive taste. When I opened my eyes the crowd seemed altered, but I couldn't tell in what way. To get my bearings, I turned back toward the bar. An impressive array of bottles glowed beneath a large neon sign of slippery cerulean script:

The Next Bardo

I wanted to meet the letter writer, the owner of the bar, to understand what was happening to me, and sought the bartender to point him out. Each step I took toward the bar lightning struck and the music changed: big band swing and men danced with women but at the bar only made eyes at each other. Disco and the familiar heat of too many bodies in too small a place as thin but muscular men in jogging shorts and tight T-shirts jostled me and each other, eyes afire with lust and the momentary glory of all the right drugs; light jazz tinkled like rain as a quiet group of Japanese men were served Suntory in sake cups by a heavily powdered geisha drag queen; sweaty sailors spun one another to live piano accompaniment. Overwhelmed, scared, I was shaking and cold, as if in the grips of a delirious fever, yet I was desperate to make it to the bar. Throughout it all, the bartender calmly cleaned a glass. Another step and the bar was nearly empty. *Can't Take My Eyes Off Of You,* by Boys Town Gang, gently pounded through the room and I sensed that I was now in the *actual* Next Bardo, as it must have existed in my youth. Most of the men had mullets or that super butch short-short hair and mustaches, Levis and T-shirts. Remembering I had a full glass in my hand, I drank deeply, hoping the potion would return me to the Ladybug's or better yet to my hotel room.

A new song slithered out of the jukebox: late-period Sylvester, raw soul with a sly rattlesnake beat. I took another step toward the bar and the song remained the same. Boys danced close together, sharing cigarettes, gripping each other's waists. Relieved that reality was no longer shuffling past like a dropped deck of cards, I opened my mouth to ask the bartender a question when Franklin grabbed my arm. He hadn't aged a day. I was about to say as much but the coldness of his hand extinguished such a foolish thought.

Of course he hasn't aged, he's... I recoiled from his icy hold. Astonishingly, he thrust his hands into the pockets of his over-sized camouflage jacket in response. *He's still shy! Did he write the letter?* I recalled that in high school he wore this jacket often, though it was rarely cold, even in winter. Bashfully, he hung his head. Touched, I reached out to reassure him but couldn't bring myself to actually touch him.

"I'm sorry," He muttered. "I didn't expect to see *you* here, I had no idea you were one of us." He looked at me with the most imploring eyes; I gulped my drink while trying to think of something to say. For years, I had wanted to apologize to Franklin, for withholding a youthful friendship that should have been natural, easy, and lifelong. *Life*. From beneath the cloud of alcohol and fear an unsure memory surfaced: was it a Greek myth? *If you eat or drink something in the underworld, you are doomed to stay there.* I put my drink on the bar and pushed it away. Franklin blinked up at me, expectant, eternally youthful.

"I'm sorry, Franklin, I'm so, so sorry I wasn't a better friend back then. It's just that in high school I was so afraid of myself and you…" A look of shock and horror had overcome him. He shook with anger. I redoubled my efforts.

"It was all my fault, I'm sorry, but I've been 'out' since college. I write about gay travel, but its honest writing, I mean I try…" It was my turn to be shocked. Franklin was rapidly changing; he shrunk skeleton thin while black Kaposi lesions spidered across his face and ate his eyes. All the while he screamed in deepening agony. I had misunderstood him. When he had stated that he had no idea I was one of them, he simply hadn't realize that I was actually still alive.

I spun away to the safety and shelter of the bathroom. It was now full of groping men making out; the room was filled with a palpable, hellish heat. Nearly delirious, I rushed the one unoccupied stall, locked the door and sat on the toilet with my head in my hands. I cried as quietly as I could while outside in the bar the 45 in the jukebox changed. King's *Love and Pride* leaked through under the door with martial, poppy cheer.

The janitor poked me in the ribs with the end of his mop and woke me up; I nearly slipped off the toilet seat but the stall was so narrow that I caught myself in time. Good thing, too, as vomit pooled on the floor between my out-stretched legs. At first I was angry at being so rudely awakened, but soon realized that I had passed out in the bar's bathroom. The vomit on the floor was mine; I shamefacedly murmured apologies, talking into my shoulder lest

I poison the scowling janitor with my lethal breath. I squeezed past him, confused and afraid. My head was pounding. I had no idea what time it was or where I had parked my car or if I could even drive. I just knew I wanted to get away from that place as fast as possible. As the bathroom door swung shut, I was momentarily tangled in the beads that hung from the entrance. I panicked and pulled down several strands as I clumsily bounded down the stairs, not daring to take another look at that janitor, whose shadowy shape reminded me of the cemetery caretaker I had seen locking up that small cemetery on the outskirts of Tampa just one day previously.

I've been back in New York for about a month. The newspaper accepted my article on Tarpon Springs but hasn't asked me to write anything else. I have contacted numerous magazines and publishers pitching a variety of different projects centered on Palm Springs; everything from an in-depth guidebook to hotel reviews, all well below my usual rate. Basically, I've throw as many darts as possible hoping for a bull's-eye. If nothing materializes, I'll just use my money from *Best Gay Bars Ever* to take a vacation. I need to get to the desert as soon as possible. I need a change of scene and an assignment to focus on. Something long-term. Mostly, I crave the heat. Since I've returned from Florida I just haven't been able to get warm. No matter how many hot showers or runs in Central Park—I've had this permanent chill.

My ex-boyfriend and I have been talking on the phone quite a bit lately. I initiated the first call; not that I told him about my recent experiences, I did not call him for that reason. I thought the sound of his voice would warm me up. It didn't, at least not yet. But we've fallen into a semi-regular routine of calling, checking in on one another. If a Palm Springs assignment pans out or if I just *go*, I think I'll invite him along. The only problem is what to do about all the mail. Since I've come back, I'm getting more and more letters about establishments long gone, a flood of maps to forgotten places. Daily letters, some from other countries in languages I can't read. Not that I've opened any of them. I don't need to. They all say the same thing. In cursive whispers: *remember for me.*

A deep felt thanks to Steve Berman for encouraging this collection and making it happen and to Craig Gidney for the skillful editing and guidance. Thanks to Sean Meriwether for accepting my first published story, included here, and for the invaluable advice and friendship that followed. Additional thanks goes to Jim Currier for sharing his literary compass, to Ian Titus for sharing stories, drinks, tears, music, masks and dreams, to Rob Stephenson for good counsel and great taste. Thanks to Richard Labonte for my first appearance in an anthology. My sincere appreciation goes to Mike and Kristen Faivre for their long friendship, the webwork and the single best advice I have ever received: "Just move up here, the rest will work itself out." Immeasurable thanks to Maria Guarascio for carefully editing far more stories than a normal friendship would allow. Thank you, Kate Shanley, for holding my hand on the dark days and sharing with me your brightest. Thanks to Jesus Acevedo for poetic navigation in the nighttime world. Thanks, Jay Suherwanto, for being so damned focused, you inspire me. Thanks to Nancy and Kristin for giving me the keys to city and to Willie for opening so many doors. Thank you, Pam, for early encouragement and downtown picnics. Special thanks to Joe, for pulling a rabbit out of the hat. Long overdue thanks are owed to Ange; those notes we passed in Latin class started this whole thing.

Thank you, Kitholeo Lai, my love, for designing
the cover of this book.